A Yearly Horror Anthology

HORRORMAXX
VOL. 1

Four Stories by H.T. Boyd

Second Edition (2026)

ISBN: 979-8-9911058-0-4

TABLE OF CONTENTS

THE ONLY HOUSE ON CHANTICLAIR LANE

"Glazer residence," I answer the phone, curling its pigtail wire around the first finger of a hand of freshly painted nails.

I hear nothing.

I put a li'l extra cheese on my voice just in case it's a potential client. "Hello? — Glazer Residence, You've got Narcissa the Babysitter—"

No response. I'd hang up, but I hear snapping and clicking on the other end. Must be a phone booth or a long-distance call. No doubt Mr. Glazer would be pissed if I hung up on somebody important.

"Hello, can I take a message?"

More clicking. Some faraway muttering. Suddenly there's a pop and a whir like a tape rewinding.

I hear a pair of raspy lungs, they talk directly into the speaker, "*I-need-you-to-listen-very-carefully.*"

The voice is thick and guttural, this is the voice of a dead man, a body in a coffin. It's flecked with dust and cobwebs.

"*Jeffery-and-Alouette Glazer-are-dead,*" the voice says.

"Oh—Shit!" I say. I smack my own forehead. "Oh shit— Oh my God that's— that's so-so-so-so fucked!"

There's a hard pause, it's filled with more static.

I grab my forehead. "Shit—sorry—for the—for the language—that's just—that's so awful—was it a car accident?"

The Rot-Mouth huffs air. My mind wanders to what the rest of my night looks like; babysitting for an orphan. I wonder if I'll still get paid.

"Hello?"

"*No.*"

"No, what?"

"*No. It-wasn't-a-car-accident.*"

I hold the telephone wire to my chest. "Oh. Okay. Well, what happened?"

"*I-killed-them.*"

It feels like someone's tossed my heart into a deep fryer. My mouth falls open, my limbs are suddenly spread with Novocaine.

"I'm—I'm sorry?"

Old Rot-Mouth really bides his time, keeps me at the edge of my couch cushion.

He speaks fast, "*I-killed-Jeffery-and-Allouette Glazer. I-need-you-to-listen-very-carefully. Failure-to-heed-the-following-instructions-properly-will-result-in-your immediate-death.*" Now he speaks slowly, "*Do you understand me?*"

"Oh, um—Yeah—tote—totally."

"*We-do-not-wish-to-harm-an-innocent-person-such-as-yourself, but-if-at-any-moment-you-stray-from-the-tasks-assigned-of-you—or-if-you-in-any-way-impede-our-mission-tonight, you-will-be-terminated-by-my-associates-waiting-outside-the-Glazer home.*"

I'm baffled. This is a prank, surely. Surely this isn't real. This is some sick puppy with a crush on me— or a disgruntled sitter who used to work under me. It's Butterfingers Ben. Or it's Gabriel from Chemistry II. Or it's a deranged talk radio prank. Whatever it is— It's not this— it's not *really* this. Jeff and Alouette aren't dead. I'm not a hostage. No. This only happens in movies.

The tension finally breaks and I laugh. "Who is this?"

"*Ask-another-question-like-that-and-you-will-be-punished.*"

I uncurl the telephone wire from my finger. The TV turns over to a commercial break, an ad for tampons of all things. I watch a woman's hand, clean, pale skin; it dunks a cotton stick into a cup of blue water. The tampon sucks it all up and transforms into this soggy blue cylinder.

"*Do-you-understand?*" Rot-Mouth asks.

"I—Sure—Yeah," my ear gets hot.

"*My-associates-waiting-outside-the-house-are-in-possession-of-a-police-scanner. If-at-any-time-you-notify-the-authorities, we-will-know-*

and-he-will-rush-into-the-home-and-terminate-you-long-before-any-police-can-arrive— Do you understand?"

"Yeah—*terminate me—*"

Jesus. Someone just threatened to *terminate* me. I've never gotten that one before.

"*My-associates-are-closely-watching-the-exits-to-the-home. Should-you-attempt-to-flee-the-Glazer-residence-before-your tasks-are completed-they-will-see-and-you will be promptly terminated. Do you understand? — — — I-need-to-hear-you-say-that-you-understand. I-need-your-word.*"

"Yeah, I—"

The phone jumps out of my grip, tumbling hard onto the black marble floor—*Shit. Fuck. Goddam it. Tits. Fuck. Ass shit. Fuck. Double goddam it.*

I squat to the ground to try to retrieve the phone but my hands aren't my hands anymore; they're covered in fear butter; they're wrapped in these pudgy trauma oven mitts. I might as well have been stung by bees.

—

Ever since I started babysitting, all anyone could say to me was how scary it must be. I have other babysitters who work under me too, and when they're first starting out, all they will talk about is how scared they are for the first few gigs. After the kid goes to sleep, they'll just sit around in the dark, driving themselves up a wall as they wait for the exact kind of phone call I just got.

I specifically blame horror movies for this. Just like they ruined camping, clowns, ventriloquist dolls, summer camps and hotels— horror movies lent this undue creepiness to an entirely boring enterprise. I mean, don't get me wrong. I love a good horror movie. Especially the ones that open with the ceremonial dismemberment of a babysitter—some young, innocent thing getting slashed to confetti and strawberry syrup in the shower — or thumbtacked to the wall by a machete—but, thus far, here, in the real world, babysitting has been an easy ride. Stressful, maybe, at times, but, like I said, *boring* more often than not, and, I haven't been dismembered or disemboweled by boring— and I've been at this for a long time. Almost four years now.

While everyone else from my graduating class went off to the coast to bury themselves in student loan debt, I expanded an already thriving 'sitting-empire'. I sit houses. I sit kids. Occasionally I sit dogs and cats. I do these things for rich people mostly and in a week of sitting-on-my-ass, I probably make as much money as a plumber. And, like I said, I also pimp out a few high school girls who do sitting for me. I've been told maybe that's the wrong word for it, *pimping*, but they sit, under my good name, and I collect twenty percent. It's a rock solid hustle.

I've made great money; fantastic money, and talk about vacation time; *I get paid to vacation*, every summer and winter break, I get a handful of multi-day, or even multi-week housesitting gigs for people who use seasons as an adjective. That's hundreds of dollars in my pocket to occupy an empty home. Money earned by taking baths in luxury bathrooms and meandering about gardens like some nineteenth century princess—or pilfering the all-you-can-eat snack pantries of the wealthy, which are, more often than not, better stocked with snacks than your standard 7-Eleven.

Up until this phone call I've had the sweetest gig in all existence; a no-horror-movie type experience. No kids possessed by the devil, no basement ghosts, no chainsaw wielding intruders. There's the occasional creepy dad who's a little too eager to walk me to my car, I guess, but that just comes with the territory.

Don't get me wrong, some bad shit has happened here and there— Once Krystal Fishcher of 4045 Mockingbird choked on a grape, but I Heimlich maneuvered that shit. Another time I was cat-sitting for an old couple on Mulberry, and one of their cats died on my watch—but—that cat was, like, forty years old or something. I mean, it was nothing—*like this*— it wasn't horror movie bullshit; a double homicide and a death threat from a man with worms in his Adam's apple.

—I guess the luck had to run out eventually. I've just had it too good for too long, and what a more fitting gig for it to all go shit than this one; the Glazers and their creepy glass mansion at 7109 Chanticlair Lane. *The Only House on Chanticlair Lane*, they call it. I've also heard kids call it *The Dollhouse* or *The Glass House* or the *Mirror House*. And I think some kids actually call it *The Last House On Chanticlair Lane*, but that name doesn't make sense. I'm sure there's even more '*spooky-word*'-hyphen-'*house*' names that I just haven't encountered yet.

Point is: it's a creepy-ass house.

Some context: a few years back, a developer tried building a neighborhood of luxury houses out here on Chanticlair Hill. About thirty minutes west from civilization; *over the river and through the* woods kind of shit.

The developer only built one house though. This one (the one I might be *terminated* in). It's a spec house meant to draw investors into the neighborhood, and, well, it didn't draw any investors.

Now 7109 Chanticlair Lane is something of an oddity; a strange, abandoned place atop a hill. The road here is freshly paved asphalt, it winds upwards through thirteen plots of razed land where the neighboring homes were never, well, *raised.*

Kids like to say—and believe me, I babysit, so I know every boogeyman local legend from the supposed serial killer who works at the Stovington's meat department to the legends of the monkey man who walks the streets at 3 A.M.—that a Manson-sex-devil-cult lives here or, that the house is a front for an underground genetics laboratory creating super soldiers. None of these things are true (I pray), but of course, rumors persist because A) kids are stupid and B) this house is generally off-putting atop its empty hill in the otherwise vacant pinewoods.

—What eats me is: I wasn't even supposed to be here tonight. Annabelle, one of my best and brightest sitters, is on the schedule, but she gets quote-unquote *bad vibes* from the long, woodsy drive out of town. So, here I am.

The babysitter in the— fuckkkinngg— horror movie with a murderer outside and a dead man talking to me on the phone.

It takes me a shamefully long time to pick the phone back up, and the longer it takes me the more nervous I get that someone is going to walk in the front door and splatter my brains onto the TV screen.

—But I manage to retrieve it. I pull the plastic brick back to my ear.

"Hello?" The Rot-Mouth asks.

"Sorry—I dropped the phone—you have to understand, mister—this is all—new to me, sir, this is my first time as a hostage, I am… I am scared totally shitless."

"That's-alright," he says, strangely sweet. *"We-do-not-wish-to-kill-you-Narcissa. You-are-unwanted-collateral. Follow-our-instructions-closely-and-you-will-walk-away-with-your-life."*

I sink down into a black leather cushion. The TV is playing a promotion for a detective show now. A handsome, mustached cop fires a flashy silver magnum at a bad guy. God, I wish I had a big mustache and a gun or a detective with those things to hide behind.

"I'm—uh—I'm listening," I tell the man.

"You-will-complete-these-tasks-in-the-exact-order-that-I-give-them-to-you. Task The First: You-will-go-into-the-private-bathroom-of-Mr.-And-Mrs.-Glazer; in-the-master-bath-vanity-you-should-discover-a-bottle-of-Zolixa. You-will-take-out-two-capsules-and-administer-them-to-the-Glazer's-son, Tommy. Do   you   understand?"

"Drug the baby, got it."

"Should-you-need-to, you-may-take-half-of-a-Zolixa-yourself-to-calm-your-nerves, but-the-choice-is-entirely-yours."

"Okay; glad you're looking out for me."

"Task-The-Second. You-will-go-to-the-laundry-room-and-you-will-tear-out-the-drywall-on-the-left-hand-side-adjacent to-the-home's-rear-exit-door. Removing-this-drywall-will-reveal-a-hidden-safe. You-will-enter-the-following-combination. Commit-it-to-your-memory: Twelve—Twenty-Seven—Seventy-Nine."

"Hold on—I've got a pen—let me—let me just—can you say the numbers again?—"

"*Twelve – Twenty-seven – Seventy-Nine.*"

With a pen once used for tonight's crossword puzzle, (well let's be honest, the celebrity word search) I scribble the numbers onto my left hand, looping them around my thumb.

"*Upon-opening-the-safe-you-will-take-its-contents-and-place-them-into-a-sack-or-bag.*"

"Okay, okay. Super-duper."

I say this to a man, a crazed murderer, like I'm helping him plan a bake sale. Oh God, do I have Stockholm Syndrome? Already? Or have I just hardwired my brain to always talk in customer service voice?

He stalls again, I guess he's surprised at how well I'm taking things.

"*This-brings-us-to-the-Third and final task. By-the-time-you-have-collected-the-contents-of-the safe, Tommy-Glazer-should-have-fallen-into-a-sedated-sleep-state. You-will-take-Tommy-and- the-safe's-contents-and-bring-them-to-my-associate-waiting-outside-the-home. So-long-as-you-do-not-do-anything-outside-of-these-instructions, you-will-not be-harmed.*"

I whistle air, a sound someone might make before they plunge into a cold pool. "Alright—So, drug the kid. Find the safe. Open it. Empty into a— into a— a bag or something. Bring the kid and the money bag to your — what did you call him? Your associate?"

"*This-is-correct—*"

I hear a second voice, another man with a rotten, guttural, fish-man voice.

"*Did you tell her the time limit?*" He asks.

It's only now I realize they're talking through a voice modulator. Of course it's a voice modulator. No one really sounds so organically demonic.

"*Oh! Yes,*" The original Rot-Mouth says. "*You-have-twenty-minutes. The-timer-will-begin-now. Fail-to-complete-these-tasks-in-time-and-my-associate-will-storm-the-home-to-complete-the-tasks-himself.*"

"—And-and—kill me—also—*sorry*—I have to assume."

"*Yes—he will kill you.*"

"Okay—I just wanted to confirm that little detail—so—uh, wish me luck, then, I guess."

I grab my own face in shame. '*Wish me luck'?*

And the fucker actually says it. "*Good-luck.*"

The conversation ends with a hard click.

—

The timer starts. But, first things first, I have to wake my feet up. They're shocked white. It feels like they're full of sand. The nails are freshly painted on the left, the right are unpainted with cotton balls between the toes. This is what I was doing when I received the call. Feels like centuries ago, now.

My stomach hurts. My head is full of bubbles and static electricity — It feels like a dream. I hate it when people say that. They always say it when something bad happens. But damn it if it isn't true. I feel like I'm dreaming, and, God, what I wouldn't do to just perk up from a nap.

I manage to stand. I try to catch my breath. I try not to fall over.

My bare feet sound like globs of playdough dropping on a basketball court as I lightly sprint around this unmercifully quiet house.

So, s'more context: there's a reason they call 7109 Chanticlair *The Dollhouse* and the *Glass House* and a few of the other nicknames. It's not *just* that it's in the middle of nowhere on a creepy hill. Whatever psychopath architect designed this place went for a weird art-deco-modernist design thingy (look; I'm a babysitter, not an architect, I don't know the fancy *philosophy of construction* terms). The insides have no doors. It's all open concept; and that concept consists mostly of swirling black marble floors and ultra-minimalist furniture that looks like anal probe devices straight off the bridge of a UFO. The art that hangs on these untextured walls is all *fru-fru* post-Jackson Pollock stuff; it's blood splatter and yellow specks, a maroon cloud on empty gray dust. The portrait that hangs above the fireplace, where a family portrait might normally hang, is a lonely framed canvas offering nothing but a splash of blue water like from the tampon commercials.

This whole place is a modern art museum-rat-maze—But really—it's the exterior of 7109 that's the spectacle. The house is composed of three sugar cube boxes of white stone; their collective front is one colossal glass window that spans every wing, every room.

When you pull up on the house during the day it's like a gigantic black mirror, but, by night, it's a dissected plaything; a house cut in half. A toy. A, well, *dollhouse*. If there are any lights on whatsoever, an outsider can see nearly everything in the front facing rooms, and I mean everything, every Edison light bulb, every bottle of liquor on the wet-bar shelves, every oblong, seventy dollar throw pillow.

So, now, I walk upon cold marble floors, trying to remember how to do it naturally. *Heel to toe. Heel to toe, Narcissa.* I arrive in a dining room where a chandelier that costs more than my car hangs over a dining table that probably costs more than my house. As I approach my own reflection in the wall-spanning window-mirror, I'm sure that, if Rot-Mouth is to be believed, whoever is parked at the end of the lawn can see every freckle on my face and every hair follicle on my head.

I have to squint and focus beyond my own eyeballs. Sure enough, beyond the slope of an immaculate emerald lawn, beyond a border of cubed hedges—there are two headlights on a beat up van; a painter's van. A big gray thing with a square face and rust on the body— it's the exact kind of thing you'd expect a killer/kidnapper to ride around in. I try to read the license plate but—dammit—I can't read. I'm too terrified to read. I've been scared straight into illiteracy.

The van flashes its brights.

It's a message. A very clear one; *get moving*. They honk the horn. It's the second half of the message— *or we'll kill you.*

I wave. I don't know why I wave. But I wave. A little hello to the people who will shoot me in the head if I fuck up.

I have to stop trying to make people like me.

—

On terrified jelly legs, I head for the grand staircase at the home's entrance. It doesn't help me any that the staircase is made to look like hovering platforms of dark chocolate candy bars. It gives me vertigo. It makes me nauseous, even in non-life-or-death scenarios.

There's no guard rail either, so I stumble upwards like a newborn baby deer, hurling my gangly legs to get to the Glazer's bedroom door.

Zolixa, I say to myself, *Zolixa, Zolixa.*

Feed the pills to Tommy.

Tear down the wall in the laundry room.

Find the safe. Enter the code. 12.27.68.

No. I check my new temporary tattoo; *Seventy-nine.* It's probably the Glazer's anniversary. Oh, of course it is, today is December 27th and they're out tonight for their anniversary dinner. Oh—*and how sad is that?* —I think; the Glazers getting murdered on their anniversary—and it's so close to Christmas. Who wants to die so close to Christmas?

Fuck. I stop as I put my hand on the door to the master.

It occurs to me that Jeff and Alouette are dead people. I mean, I already knew that, but I guess the fact of it finally sinks in through the shock. I had just seen Jeff and Alouette. They'd been two people, you know, humans, real alive human beings with skin and faces and buttholes and hopes and dreams. I'd watched them descend those very same hovering chocolate bar stairs, what was that? Three hours ago? A little less?

Jeff was in a white jacket tuxedo and Alouette was in a sparkling blue ball gown. They were going into the city; to some sushi place where a plate of sashimi is like 8000 trillion dollars, and afterward some minimalist Philip Glass concerto in the park—and the two of them—they were so, well, not just alive, but so pretty and so rich, and they were so bubbly-shiny-young in that way rich people are always bubbly-shiny-young. And they were alive. They were alive, and now, they're what, they're *dead?*

Made to be dead. *Killed* is the word, I have to remind myself. *Murdered.*

I have to wonder, what did the Rot-Mouth do to them? Run their town car off a bridge? Poison their dinner? Cut the cables on an elevator—No, it's the real world, not a cartoon. Someone probably just shot them in their heads. God. That's *so* horrible. I hope it didn't hurt. They were such nice people. Alouette was so pretty. She was from South Africa and had a little French-African accent. I mean, let's be clear, her family made their fortune on blood diamond mines, but, she was a nice lady!—and she was still somebody's mom—and, I mean, Jeff was a total creep. Like, five alarm cleavage starer, sociopath, chuckling at his own creepy jokes, but, oh, he didn't deserve to be capped like some dog with rabies. Oh no. Oh God and they paid me so much money! And I just know my brain is gonna be so fucked up if I survive this.

—

I soldier forth. I regain control of the meat suit that is my body and I push into the Glazer's bedroom.

The master bedroom of this house has always reminded me of a lair for an evil ice witch. It's got these snow white carpets and the walls are this snow white sand-stone. A chandelier is composed of eight descending snow crystals, illuminated by bulbs at their bases; it hangs right over a bed hole. Yes, a *bedhole.* For reasons I cannot comprehend, instead of a regular furniture bed, there's a square hole in the room's center; a sort of subterranean bird's nest. It's filled with pink silk blankets and these strange fish-scale-patterned body pillows. I've never dwelled much on this. I once thought it was a weird sex thing, but, really, I just think rich people buy stupid things, like bedholes, to feel special.

I move past this; there isn't the time to consider a dead couple's bed. I get to the bathroom and stumble to a place above a strange cylindrical-pot toilet where a medicine cabinet hangs. I rip it open, and as it was so foretold, there's an amber bottle of Zolixa. I'm still shaking so bad I struggle to get past the child-proof locking, but when I do I salt-shaker out a handful of pills.

They're an off-white baby blue, the color of sleep.

Old Rot-Mouth gave me permission to have one. I consider it. I really do. Some drugs sound absolutely amazing right now, but, no, I shouldn't. I can't. What if I faint? What will happen then? I'll die in my sleep. That's awful. I would die not even knowing I was dying.

—

It doesn't quite hit me what I'm doing until I'm opening the door to Tommy's room.

Here I am, some hideous arm of a criminal enterprise, an accomplice, with a handful of knock-you-out drugs, sneaking into the bedroom of a sleeping child.

I don't turn on the light. I don't want to scare him.

While everything else in this house is sterile and menacing like a doctor's office, Tommy's room is very much the opposite. It's a technicolor daycare of toys and books; it's all round corners and foam and smiling faces. I have to navigate carefully around wooden train tracks, rubber monsters, and stuffed animals whose voice boxes would surely talk if I stepped on them the wrong way.

Tommy is too old for a crib, but he sleeps in one regardless. He has a mobile of spinning plastic dinosaurs. I find him in their trance, a lump in the dark, no clue in his little head what's happened to his mom and dad. His hilariously long eyelashes wriggle softly as he adjusts into a new sleeping position. He's already out cold.

I imagine it. I imagine my task. I imagine taking the pills in my palm and waking up this dreaming child and feeding him drugs so he can be easily transported and shipped off in the back of a creepy painter van.

It's all so totally *ew*.

They're kidnapping him, I assume, for the maternal grandparents' ransom money. See; Jeff Glazer, he's not poor by any means; him and his brother, Charlie, are orthodontists. They developed a new kind of minimally invasive headgear for braces. I mean, they're not gonna buy their own island with braces money, but they're quite comfortable. Alouette, on the other hand, is where the money really comes from—or rather came from, I guess. She's dead now. I have to keep reminding myself this.

Alouette Glazer, formerly Alouette Argestes, came from the Argestes family—(ever heard the expression, *pawn your testes, buy Argestes*?) – well, their company slogan is literally just *THE BEST DIAMONDS* if that gives you a hint about what they do. It was a big deal when Alouette came to our town, and, well, it shouldn't surprise you to hear she *does* have private island money. I mean her family quite literally has a private island. Two, in fact. One is near Costa Rica and the other is off the coast of Maine (I think, I could be wrong, it might have been Virginia—but—but this really doesn't matter right now).

It's awful. It's all so awful. Not the private island part, the kidnapping. I'm sure if they cut off little Tommy Glazer's big toe and mailed it to Grandmama and Grandpapa Argestes in South Africa, they would pay the equivalent of Canada's GDP for his safe return.

Gross. Wealth is gross. Money is gross. You know what I think? I think there probably wouldn't be crimes like this if we just made it a little less terrible to be poor. If we just had nationalized healthcare, and better wages for teachers, and if we had food recycling programs that took all the food waste from restaurants and repurposed them for food banks. My friend Zara works at a restaurant and do you know how much edible food goes in the garbage every day?

Focus on the task, Narcissa.

In the dark, I stand over Tommy with two Zolixa pills, their sugar skins smudging blue in my palm.

The kid bites his lower lip. Little orphan. My little orphan. Just an hour ago I was reading him a book about a stuffed bear who came to life. My eyes swell up.

Tommy is—well, he's three. There's not a lot to a three year old. He's blonde. Pampered. He hates hairdryers. Hates the sound of a toilet flushing. He likes anything with dinosaurs, and he seems awful fond of pizza—or more accurately, he likes to smash pizzas with his tiny pink fists.

I imagine force-feeding this sweet, spoiled, overgrown toddler a near lethal dose of benzos and it just—it just defiles the integrity of my babysitting empire.

—I don't do it. I don't dose the kid. They won't know, I promise myself. He'll be confused. He'll be sleepy. It's not like they're going to drug test him to confirm I did it. I mean, what if he dies? What if two pills is too many and he doesn't wake up? That's a dead kid on my hands. Not on the kidnappers.

I kind of move my hands toward his mouth, you know, in case they can see. In case they're watching, (certainly they can see me, one whole wall of this room is made of glass)—but it's not like they can see a pill from two hundred feet away. So, when the act is over I toss the sleeping pills into a pile of stuffed animals and I flee.

—

"Step Two," I say it out loud, now, "The safe—"

When I venture down the stairs I give a big goofy thumbs up to the van waiting outside. I really try to sell it—*yep, I just gave that kid the pills! You could drop a brick on him and he wouldn't even flinch!*

My mind's eye is forced to imagine whoever it is that's out there in the van. I hate to stereotype, but I imagine a guy in a wifebeater, and he's probably got a gold chain necklace. Maybe he's smoking a cigar and he's got KID and NAP tattooed across his knuckles. Maybe he's a professional kidnapper. Maybe he went to college at Kidnapping University where he majored in ransom letters and minored in ether rag soaking.

Focus! Narcissa, Focus!

I get to the laundry room, adjacent to the kitchen and rear exit.

Even the Glazer's laundry machines are these bizarre sci-fi warp engines with keyboards and digital displays. God, I just don't get it—but, I focus on my mission. The sooner I empty the safe, the sooner I can hand the kid off and— if these thieves are to be believed— the sooner I can be done with this bullshit.

I hit the eye-level drywall by the rear exit door with my bare fist, but this hurts. Quite a lot, actually. Realizing I need a better strategy, I take a broom and I smash at the wall like it were a piñata. Once I've hit a decent hole, I begin to peel away at the chunks of drywall. It breaks off in big shards, the way a graham cracker breaks, and the dust forces me to sneeze. I pull more and more wall away and reveal the home's ugly guts of electrical wires and framing wood and that pink cotton candy stuff that keeps the cold out.

Sure as the Zolixa was predicted, I find a safe. It's at my nose level, about two feet from the rear exit door frame. It's a thin, beige box; a brown logo on the door reads, in italicized words: *SAFE 'N' SOUND PREMIUM.*

It's an electric safe, one with a numerical keypad. *How fancy*, I think, *how high tech*. And thank God because my panicked hands could not manage a spinning dial right now. I put in the combination: 12. 27. 79. It beeps. A green light flashes. It clicks. I pull the handle.

A small part of me can't help but feel excited, *hey*, hidden wall treasure is still hidden wall treasure *am-I-right*? I dream of all the things that could be inside; documents from the CIA? A jar with alien eggs, maybe, like, a splinter of the cross they crucified Jesus with?

Of course, the safe's contents consist of nothing but velvet black bags. I open one up and the inside shines like a glitter-soaked birthday card. It confirms my suspicion; it's diamonds. Bags and bags and *bags* of diamonds. This is a safe in the house of an heir to the Argestes family, after all, it makes sense.

I could pocket one, I think. The laundry room is mostly hidden behind the kitchen; it's one of the few spots where I am totally obscured from the front yard van watcher. I could probably put a whole bag in my pocket and no one would notice—but—then again—the police might, and maybe they'll think I was in on it—and they'd probably arrest me. And jail doesn't sound very nice.

So, with no reward for myself, I scramble for the kitchen and tear into a trash can where there's a marinara stained shoe box (for a new pair of men's ski boots). It's kind of the perfect size, really, and the pizza sauce lends it an element of disguise. You know, who is gonna think there's millions of dollars in diamonds contained in a sauce stained shoe box?

So, I go to the safe and dump in every diamond bag. It fits. Perfectly. Even in the chaos you have to appreciate the little things. It's like the shoe box was made for the contents of that safe. I put the top back on. Tuck it under my arm.

A sound erupts behind me. It's ear-splitting loud; a sound like—like a sneezing robot. It's nothing short of a miracle that I don't shit my pants then and there. It's the phone. The damn Glazers couldn't have a normal phone with a normal bell ringer. No. They have a rich people high-tech electronic phone that rings with a noise like a warbling ray-gun.

On pure instinct I go for the receiver before it can reach the second ring.

"Hello?" I beg.

"Good evening, this is Officer Weathers with the Trimbur County Sheriff's Department."

Do I hang up? Should I hang up? I should absolutely hang up.

"Hello?" the officer asks again.

"Uhhh, hi," I say, and then shake my head vapidly, trying to kickstart my brain.

"Who, may I ask, am I speaking to?" the officer now says.

I should hang up, but, my mouth just starts going off without my brain's approval. "This is Narcissa Ruiz— I'm babysitting for the Glazer's tonight."

I dart my eyes at the gaping windows at the front of the house. There's nothing to see there, only a mirror, but, there're men, *killers*, lurking beyond that mirror and they're watching my every move. No doubt they can see the colossal phone at my ear.

I cover my mouth and bury my neck into my shoulders, I turn around and head back to the cover of the laundry room.

I continue, "Is there—a—problem?""

"I'm afraid so, ma'am. There's been an incident. We're afraid Alouette and Jeffery Glazer are dead."

I really do try to sound surprised, like this isn't the second time I'm hearing this information, "Oh."

"We believe they have been the victim of a car bombing."

"OH!" Now I really am surprised.

"Aloutette died en route to the hospital, but Jeffery got the worst of it. He's been marred beyond recognition—we'll have to identify him with dental records—"

Those are some colorful details, officer Weathers, I think, but don't say.

He continues. "We're sorry to do this to you, but we'll be sending an investigation unit out to the Glazer residence in the next hour or so. Can you monitor the property until then?"

"Uh—yes, of course," I stammer. "—An hour sounds fine, totally fine, but, could you maybe get here a little sooner? Like—immediately, maybe even?"

"Is there a problem?" The cop asks.

Oh, I should shut up. I should shut up. I should absolutely shut up the mouth that is on my face.

But I don't. "Yeah," I nod. "There's a pretty big problem out here."

"Lock the doors we'll send a—"

POP! GEEEUUUSSHHH.

Gunshot! Gunshot! GUNSHOT! It's a gunshot I'm sure of it. Everything goes real bright and then everything goes completely black.

The phone falls from my hand, the diamond box falls from my elbow crook. I let out a death-shriek. I feel around my chest for fresh and bleeding holes. Am I dead? I'm dead, aren't I? Jesus, this isn't the afterlife, is it? Just blackness and my own endless thoughts? Hell would be preferable to this. *Is this hell?* Just my own inner-monologue on a blank slate?

My eyes adjust. I make the shape of a kitchen; the laundry, all shrouded in black and gray-blue. I guess it wasn't a gunshot, it was the power shutting off. I'm relieved, but only for about the single second of realization that I'm not a corpse. Terror returns in the second following where I realize that someone has purposefully shut off the power. I peak my head out of cover. Beyond the foyer and dining room, where there was once a giant mirror, there is now a true, gaping view-hole into the night. Beyond it, framed by the stars and faraway black pinewoods, the kidnapper's van sits beyond the hedges; its headlights off. Its driver's seat empty.

Rot-Mouth and Rot Mouth's associate, they're coming for me. I can't see them, but they're out of their van and they could be anywhere.

Shit. Fuck. Stupid. Fucking. Goddam. Rich. People. Spooky house. Shit gig. Shit Business. Fucking midnight movie bullshit. Fucking Annabelle canceling because she's scared of the woods. Bullshit!

Scrambling, I hide the box of diamonds in the washing machine, just to get them out of my hands. Then, maybe it's out of some kind of maternal instinct, I don't know, but I book it for Tommy's room on the second floor, crawling up the stairs on all fours like a champion greyhound.

As soon as I get into his room I hear glass shatter downstairs. Something is coming. Something is coming to kill me, just like they promised. Now I'm going to die. I'm going to die two days after Christmas. My poor mom and dad, this is gonna ruin all their future Christmases. And mine too. Because I'm going to be dead for every Christmas! Fuck. *Ew.*

I descend over Tommy's crib.

"*Naw-cissa?*" The little idiot asks as he comes awake with a strobing blink.

I manhandle the kid into my arms without any delicacy.

"Shut up," I swear. "Keep your mouth shut!"

I throw him and myself into the darkness of his walk-in closet (yes, he's three years old and has a walk-in closet). It's another mess of boxes and old clothes and stuffed animals. It's dark here. It smells like mothballs, but it feels safe.

His voice is small, it's the way a cartoon mouse talks. "*What happun?*"

"*Shut up. Just shut up. Keep your mouth shut!*"

He squirms against my chest and kicks at me.

I listen. I listen over my own pounding heart and this fidgeting orphan.

There's footsteps. They're coming up the stairs. Is it one person or two? I can't tell. I try listening for the feet, but I'm not a spy. I'm not a blind person with heightened hearing abilities—and Tommy keeps making this grunting noise. I shake him. I whisper scream into his ear to sit still.

All I hear is movement. Maybe it's one guy, maybe it's ten guys. Maybe it's the devil himself on goat hooves, I really don't know.

Whatever it is, it's in the hallway. It's getting closer.

"*Daddy said Unk'yl Chykgo'come?*" Tommy mutters some stupid squealing bird-peep question and I don't have the patience to translate.

I can only shake him, and wrap my hand around his tiny lips. "*Shsshhhuuttt up. Shut up. Shut up.*"

I decide I need a weapon. This is it. God, they're probably armed. I've never thought about how fucking terrifying a gun is until one was coming down the hallway for me. It's always machetes and knives in the movies— I wish I was being attacked by someone with a machete or a knife. I'd have a chance at least. What is a gun if not just an off-switch for my circulatory system?

Closer. Closer. Closer.

"*Is'Ch—*" Tommy peeps and I squeeze my hand around his stupid lips.

A weapon, I think. I reach around, quiet as I can.

There's a thin strip at the closet's base. It glows yellow as a figure walks past with a flashlight.

The invader is standing at the crib. He'll be at the closet any second. God, why did I hide here? I reach for the nearest physical object I can find. It's something wooden, boxy— nothing more than a toy. But— it's heavy—it's heavy and it's something to smack with.

The closet handle jiggles.

The door swings open, and on the other side there is only the blinding beam of a flashlight.

Tommy shrieks, I close my eyes, I wildly stab with the caboose of what turns out to be a toy train. It strikes at the empty air in front of me.

The invader shrieks himself, a low-winded, shocked grunt. His body moves. The flashlight moves. It all happens so slowly, I see a gloved hand struggling with a belt and then—silver— a tube with a hole and a hammer—is that a gun? It's a gun!

'*Pop*'. It makes a hollow noise— like a balloon or a tire popping— it's—it's followed by another shot. I watch the barrel ignite. I watch an explosion and a puff of smoke. This is the stuff that happens in nightmares, not real life. A gun is going off—*at me*. Three feet away. Impossible to stop. I see the cylinder spin. I see the muzzle flash. I smell the smoke. My hands try to catch bullets, but hands can't catch bullets.

He fires a third time and my body feels the hit.

I've been shot! My hand! My finger! My head! But, again, most importantly, my head! It's the last place you want to get shot. The bullet flew through my open hand and into my open mouth, it hit my lips, it struck my two front teeth, exploding them on impact! I have been shot with a bullet! It's like getting stung by a bee, or maybe it's more like getting fast work done by a clumsy dentist. I feel it, and I don't feel it too. There's no pain. Just a sentience of dead and burning nerves working their way into my gums and my throat.

Tommy drops from my grip. My hands cover my mouth as if I'd just been caught saying a dirty word.

The figure, this invader in black, he fires his gun a fourth time and I don't feel it. I'm already dropping for the ground.

I'm dead aren't I? Earlier was a fluke. Now, I'm really dead. For real this time. I saw the gun go off at my face. I saw a hole plop into my hand. I didn't feel the final shot because I'm dead. These are the first moments of the afterlife. There's a white ring, it builds around my peripheral vision. I'm a specter. I'm a phantom. Am I an angel? When I stand back up will I be standing over my expired corporeal form like Casper the friendly fucking ghost?

In what I assume are my last moments as a living person, I see black boots encroach on a confused Tommy, they corner him in the closet. He makes a noise like a chimp being forced into a paper shredder as he's scooped up by the black clad boogey man.

Up into his arms, Tommy goes, he tantrums, but he is a twenty-eight pound toddler and his abductor is 300 raw pounds of muscle in a ski mask.

They leave. The two of them. The sounds of boots and toddler screams fade into the hall and then down the stairs where I hear the young boy leap from his captor and give chase.

I feel the carpet against my face. I feel shattered teeth and blood gathering around my lips and chin. I taste it, I taste my mouth, it's like dirty meat on a barbecue. Pennies and grimy quarters. There's grit, like sand. It's my exploded teeth and bits of bullet. My tongue feels around and the still hot kernels of what used to be teeth.

I feel my heart—racing, ten thousand beats a second.

I guess it means I'm alive.

———

I bleed. I lie. I taste nasty tastes.

I hear the front door.

I'm really alive, aren't I? I've just taken a gunshot to the head and I'm alive. Is there a hole in my brain? Am I going to be like— *what was that guy's name?* That guy who had a train-pole-thing running through his head. *Phineas Cage?* Phineas Gauge? I guess If I can remember the obscure story of Phineas Gauge I'm probably not brain damaged. So, that's nice.

I roll my tongue around. There're missing teeth and a new hole in my face. I hold out my right hand. The hand I write with and also tried to catch a bullet with. From what I can see in the faint, gray light, the bullet went through the place where my pointer and middle finger meet. A weirdly thin blood oozes from a gnarly black hole here. I move my fingers and I see the little puppet string tendons that are supposed to be hidden by the skin.

Oh! So totally gross!

I turn my attention upward; it's hard to see in the dark, but, sure as my heart still beats, there's three bullet holes in the drywall at the far side of the closet. He shot four times and I only got shot once and—Jesus, *what a terrible aim he is*—that was point-blank range!

I pick myself up and feel around my face with my left hand, my remaining, good hand. My top lip is split evenly into two pieces at the perfect center below the nose, and— my front two teeth are—Oh, I just need to see it.

I get to my feet and race for the master bathroom. Like an idiot, I flicker the light-switch a dozen times before remembering the power's been cut. Luckily, or maybe unluckily, there's enough moonlight from the window to see my reflection in the mirror.

I'm honestly shocked there's so little blood. I mean, don't get me wrong, there's a lot of blood. There's tons of the stuff, it drips down my chin and neck and ruins my favorite yellow jumper— but, the way it felt, I was expecting Overlook Hotel elevator levels of gore. I'm still quite disfigured. I might have only gotten one bullet, but damn, that bullet got me good. There's a hole, it's in my lips, and above it too, it's a gorey absence of skin where Hitler's mustache was. Beneath it are two exploded dud-teeth that lead to a small scab of scorched gums. Other teeth are chipped, the nose is freckled with burns the size of pepper flakes. I take my left hand and feel at my upper lip—I can move the two mouthy flesh hunks independent of one another.

I won't be kissing anyone again anytime soon, I think. That's just a silly little joke. Just a joke to keep from fainting.

"Fuck!"

There's nothing else to say, my voice is wet with blood. The sound misshapen by the tear at the center of my face.

There's a noise. Downstairs. The front door opens. I squeal.

I drop to the floor as soon as I hear it. He's coming back for me.

I hear something— it's talking— he's talking. There's more than one of them!

"*—What was I supposed to do? She attacked me! It was self-defense!*"

"She was part of the story, Chuck, the narrative— the babysitter was gonna keep us insulated—clean! Sell the story! You're sure she's dead?"

—Maybe that's Rot-Mouth, the second voice, just without his scrambler—

"Four headshots, man—point-blank—God, it was terrible. I'm pretty sure I saw a part of her brain fly out! Man, her fucking brain!"

I don't know what this guy thinks he saw but my brain is still in my head, thank you very much.

"I feel awful. Aw, man, I didn't want to kill her! She babysat for me once, man. She babysat Kevin. I gave her a ride home. She was just a kid! I popped her head, man! She spooked me and I popped her fucking head! I popped her fucking head!"

"Alright—alright—keep it together, alright? She's gone! It happened. It's done. Where's Tommy?"

"I don't know, man! He bit me! He ran off!"

"He bit you?"

"He bit me! I dropped him! He ran away!"

"Jesus Christ, Chuck! Where are the diamonds!"

"I don't know!"

"Chuck!"

"I know! I know! I fucked it all up! I'm sorry!"

I don't make a sound. I tip toe into the master bedroom and just— *listen.* They hurry through the house and make their way for the laundry room.

Their voices are more faint now, but, sound has a way of echoing on those hard marble floors.

"Well, she got the safe open, but where's the payload?"

"Is it not there?"

"Are you blind; It's empty. Weren't you watching her? Did you see what she put it in?"

"No— I-I-I- I couldn't see her!"

"What do you mean— It's a glass house!"

"Yeah, and the laundry room is hidden! I don't have x-ray vision. I looked away for a second, just a second, when I looked back, she was on the phone. I thought you were in the backyard, why didn't you see it?"

"I was at the fuse box in the cellar—Goddamit, Chuck!—"

"Just forget the diamonds, man, fuck it! Let's find Tommy and we'll get out of here before the cops show up. No doubt they're already on the way!"

"There's fifty million dollars in diamonds around here somewhere, Chuck—expat cash—start over cash."

I hear boxes clatter. I hear drawers slam open and shut.

"I'll find Tommy, you go back upstairs and check the babysitter."

"—Check the babysitter! Why?!—"

"She probably had the diamonds on her, moron. Go! Go look!"

"—But—"

"Chuck, it's a dead body. She can't hurt you anymore. She probably has the loot on her; go look! NOW!"

—

BirdShit. Dogshit, Pigshit. Giraffe-shit. Goddamit. Bigfoot shit. Tits. Antichrist. Fuck it all.

Chuck, my would be murderer works the stairs. They're not easy for him either —(they really are, just, not ergonomically friendly stairs)— I try to remember all the Chucks I've babysat for. Maybe a few Charleses, a Carl here or there, a couple of Charlies, but I don't remember a Chuck—or a Kevin, for that matter. I've done a lot of babysitting, I can't remember everyone.

Either way, I watch from the shadows of the master door frame as this massive figure takes to the stairs. Puffy jacket and ski-mask, he bumbles over the high arch steps in bulky mountain boots. In ten seconds he'll be back in that closet and see that I've disappeared like Mikey Myers and he's gonna start looking for me.

I could play dead, I think OR I could jump out the window and run like hell—but these don't seem like smart options. They really just sound like ways to get shot again or break a limb.

So, I'll hide, I decide. I'll hide real good and these two idiots will find their diamonds and leave the house— they'll leave the house—*with Tommy screaming in the back of their van.*

Goddamit. I can't let a fresh orphan leave with these kidnappers.

You know, doctors take a hippocrackaddict oath, or whatever, to first, *do no harm.* I wonder if there's not a hippocrackaddict oath to babysitters. What's Latin for "*Do Not Let The Child Get Kidnapped*"?

I have to do something. Conquer while they're divided.

But what?

Chuck reaches the top of the stairs, I hear him return to Tommy's room. He whimpers to himself when he sees the empty spot of carpet where my dead body is supposed to be.

"*Oh shit,*" he cries, under his breath. "*Oh shit, oh, shit, oh shit.*"

Yeah, '*oh shit*', Chuck. The feeling is mutual.

I dive for the underside of the master bath sink. It opens with a soft squeak, but I don't think anyone could hear it. Inside is a supply of toilet paper, soap and some cleaning products. A few candles (lemongrass scented, that sounds nice).

God, Jesus Christ, I know I haven't been to Mass in eight years, but can you give a girl a revolver hidden underneath this sink? Maybe a bazooka? Or at least one of those tiny baseball bats?

I dig around. No gun. No tiny baseball bat. No bazooka.

—I watch a lot of children's programming. There's this PSA they always run with this red puppet with googly eyes—and he sings a song about not drinking the stuff under the sink. But which stuff, little puppet? Toilet bowl cleaner? Drain declogger? Spray deodorant? Why couldn't the puppet have explicitly stated which chemicals can be weaponized in an emergency situation?

I hear Chuck in the guest bedroom down the hall. I panic and I can tell from his muttering and the way he's throwing the doors that he's panicking too. At least he's too embarrassed to call for his accomplice.

The two of us are on a collision course now and neither of us are particularly fond of committing murder. This is gonna be a shit show.

C'mon. C'mon. I keep rearranging stuff in the sub sink shelves like a desperate gambler at a slot machine. Where is my assault rifle? Where is my katana?

Beside another scented candle, I find a measly plastic lighter, and with that, I grab the closest thing that says the word flammable on it.

—

Chuck yells, right outside the master, *"Hey! Have you found Tommy?"*

"What?"

"Have you found Tommy?"

"No," Rot-Mouth calls back. *"Did you get the diamonds?"*

"No— they weren't on her. Should we go?—let's just go man. Let's go."

"Two more minutes! Check the master!"

"Oh. Okay."

Chuck creeps in, "Hello?"

His gun is drawn, he holds it beside his flashlight. The beam trembles. He's more scared than I am.

"Um—Police! Uh—Police department! Please show yourself."

Yeah, nice try, what cop walks in with a ski mask, Chuck? Is this really the best you got? I watch him from my new hiding place behind an armoire as he carefully maneuvers around the bed-hole.

"Hello?"

He gently opens the door to the bathroom and whispers again, "He —Hello?"

I try to quiet my breathing. My mom made me take clarinet in middle school. I always hated it, but it taught me to inhale as I exhale; who knew Clarinet was training for guerilla warfare stealth operations.

I pop up my head from behind a boxy modern armoire. Chuck is in the bathroom. He has his back to me. He flings the shower curtain open, revealing nothing but a criminally oversized bathtub. I then catch him staring at the floor. He's studying something; It's my blood. I left plenty of it over there as the new holes in my face and hand bled during my search for a weapon.

Sweet, innocent Chuck, not an ounce of killer instinct in his little head. He sets his flashlight down—and—then—truly a miracle—he sets his revolver down too. He removes a glove and dips it into my pool of mouth blood. He tastes it.

"Blood," he says, to himself.

Yeah, Chuck, it's red and stinks like pennies. *It's blood.* Congratulations, you're a regular Nosferatu.

Hear me out, I've never wanted to kill someone before. It's not something I've ever had the inclination to do; maybe I've wanted to wring the odd brat's neck, but, I've never wanted to amputate someone's soul from their mortal coil, especially not with fire–but, my hands are kinda tied here, and, I don't want to do it half-assed like Chuck did me. I need to be confident, I remind myself—I need to be a warrior. I need to be a big mustached prime-time detective, and, now I sort of *do* have a big mustache, made of blood, so maybe I look the part.

Now, if bad babysitting gigs have taught me anything, anything at all; it's how to be scary. So, with clarinet trained lungs and five odd years of screaming at children mid-tantrum, I take a deep, powerful breath, I take in as much air as I can.

I firmly grasp my weapons and I storm Chuck's backside.

I release my breath first; I shout. Not an ordinary shout. Not a frightened girlie scream. It's more of a roar; it's a noise like a, well, like a girl who doesn't want to die, but just got shot in the face might make. Blood, spit and little bits of lead fly out on a tremendous burst of sound.

Chuck is too startled to go for his gun, but, he won't have enough time anyways. With my right hand I squeeze a bottle of nail polish remover; a thin, stinking, alcohol concentrate soaks into his ski mask, the back of his jacket and the seat of his pants.

Moving quick, I then pocket the nail polish remover, take a lighter and a bottle of spray deodorant. I learned this little trick from a brat named Lucas Marsh; the Terror of 6767 Branchland Court. Worst kid I ever sat. Who'd have thought his makeshift recipe for a flamethrower would go on to save my life.

Just as Lucas had tormented me when I was sixteen years old, I torment Chuck. With blood-wet and ripped up fingers, I snap the lighter while the other hand triggers a can of aerosol deodorant and runs the spray through the flame to make a persistent fireball.

Fire kisses Chuck, but, it's really the nail polish remover that does the job. It erupts into blue flames. Soaked wool and cotton catch fire in shades of glowing blue and green. The polyester melts.

Chuck ignites like the last firework at a Fourth of July show, and he screams like one too. I jump away. I fall backwards out of the bathroom and tumble into the bedhole, nearly breaking my neck on the frame. I scramble back to a stand. Pull myself out of the bed.

I hadn't planned any further than this. I guess I had assumed that Chuck would just explode and be dead, but, Chuck is very much alive and he's very much on fire and he's very loud and angry as he comes thrashing out of the bathroom.

Fire is on his knees. His elbows. His hands. He makes this odd, masculine, elephantine roar as he bounces and sparks, and, as he flings himself around the master bedroom like a pinball he sets little fires all around the room. He sets fire to sections of the carpet. He throws himself against a north wall curtain and sets those on fire too. He begins to strip. A glove flies off. So does a jacket. He manages to take off his mask, where a semi-recognizable face and bald head are obscured by fire. He pats himself down as he throws himself against walls.

I back into a corner, my fire starter chemicals held over my heart.

Oh, God, I have to finish him. I have to finish him off or he's going to put these fires out and choke me to death.

The first time was pure adrenaline and self defense, kicking him while he's down just feels—*cruel*. But I do it. I do it because I have to. Because if I don't, he'll eat me, or beat me, or rape me, or put me in his van and take me to another country. So, I meet him halfway as he flails towards the dresser. Before he's even seen me; I douse him with the remainder of the nail polish remover, flinging the liquid like a pope flings an aspergillum (…that's the holy water flinging thing. It's called an aspergillum. I was a Catholic. Sorry, that's just what it's called…).

The remainder of the alcohol concentrate soaks into Chuck's bare face flesh, sinking into his pores, getting into the corners of his eyes. I then ignite it with the aerosol flamethrower.

It doesn't seem real; the way Chuck's face melts into an overexcited Jack-O-Lantern; his eyes close, the mouth opens and sucks in fire. The skin melts off chunky cheeks, like rubber. The hair of his eyebrows and mustache fly upward to stinking black wires and then—dust, inside a cloud of smoke. He falls backwards, away from the fireball and into the bed pit.

Now, I don't know what kind of synthetic materials the Glazers were using to dress their bed, but, the whole pit goes up in flames. The air turns black. The room gets hot. Chuck's body stops writhing and becomes nothing more than fuel. Where once was a bed hole and a man there is now a wicked pyre that cackles and spreads for the carpet, it kisses the crystal chandelier.

The fire is loud. Movies never do it justice just how fucking loud fire can be. The cackling, the sucking whoosh, the roar.

I cough. And coughing doesn't feel nice with my face split in half and exposed nerve tissue at my missing teeth.

A little late, but the fire alarm finally goes off. I guess they're battery powered. If the fire is loud then this shit is a sonic weapon. A steady; YEEP YEEP YEEP! It rings from the ceilings and echoes off every hard surface.

I make a move for the bathroom to grab the revolver, but, fire cuts me off. It crawls onto the carpet and vomits heat at me; I nearly lose an eyebrow.

I head the other direction, for the exit to the master. I escape the room just as another body comes dashing up the stairs. The Rot Mouth. We finally meet.

He's a wintery figure, anonymous in a ski mask with only slits for eyes. He is tall, he is wide. His body is formless in puffy jacket and puffy pants.

"Narcissa?" He asks, oddly calm, oddly friendly considering how hectic this all is.

I recognize his voice. I'm sure if I were at a grocery store I could place from where, but, at the moment my mind is focused on the squealing alarm and the fire at my ass and the black tornado of smoke and the presence of another attacker.

Without much thought, I pull the flamethrower on him and just in time too, as he begins to rush me. I spray his ski mask with aerosol and hold up the lighter to bring it to flame. I snap the flint, once, twice, a third time—but, the fire never catches. *Fuck it*. What was supposed to be a flamethrower comes out as nothing but a Men's-Sports-Performance-Scented-Blinding-Juice. While not flaming, the spray still temporarily confuses the Rot Mouth. He cowers away, swearing and coughing.

I run past him. Through smoke; through ringing alarm. I jettison down the stairs, but I jettison too fast. These goddam hovering candybar stairs without a proper rail. There's no way they're up to code— my foot misses the third to last step. I go tumbling, flying into the open air, and long before I hit the ground, I know I've fucked up bad.

—

Somehow, this fall hurts so unimaginably worse than getting shot in the face. I land on the hard marble before the exit and it's like when a cartoon character gets hit with a frying pan; I see yellow stars and tiny blue birds circling around my head tweeting. It winds me. Every organ churns into a knot. I swear a new swear word that hasn't been invented yet, it's a sort of pig squeal combined with a belch and a gasp.

I hear it, *I feel it*, as a rib snaps into two pieces on impact, but it's worst at my left ankle which tried to steady the fall. Holy fuck does it hurt. Holy fuck does it hurt even worse when I try to stand up. I'm forced to perch on my right bare foot while my left toes just barely grace the ground. It's broken. It's *got to* be broken. Shit! God damn it! A bullet to the mouth, a hole in the hand, now a busted ankle and a broken rib. There's not going to be much left of me pretty soon here.

It's all so disorienting. The pain. The nightmare of this night and the house collapsing in on itself. Darkness. Fire. Smoke. The battery-powered alarms keep screaming. Up the staircase landing I see Rot-Mouth fighting his way into the master bedroom, he calls Chuck's name.

—But Chuck's dead, bitch. And, soon enough, you will be too.

—

In shadow and red firelight, I hobble.

Fire eats the second story. I don't know if it's a paint thing or an architecture thing, but this goddam house is a bundle of kindling.

I glance out the front yard and see an indifferent night. A cold lawn and a quietly resting painter's van. My own car, a yellow bug from 1964, sleeps quietly down the empty block.

Where in God's name are the cops, I wonder?

It might seem more intelligent to take my leave now from 7109 Chanticlair, but, I hop-skip-leg for the kitchen instead; I'm not going anywhere without a weapon.

I make it to onyx quartzite counters and hobble for a rack of rich-person-stainless-steel-artisan-green-marble-handed-Russian steak knives in a wooden block. I take out the butcher knife. It's practically two feet long with chrome mirrored blades.

I think about those movies. Those movies where they dismember the babysitter. She always takes the butcher knife to defend herself—but— I swear, in every one of those movies she always drops it, and to be fair,

I've dropped everything I've picked up tonight. I look at this knife, I look at my clammy, tremoring palms— and I wonder—how can I not drop it? How can I be the babysitter who does not drop the knife?

YEEP- YEEP – YEEP – YEEP. The fire alarm blares.

I open up the Glazer's utility drawer. Inside is a mess of batteries, trinkets, and Christmas cards. I open the drawer beneath it where there's loose screws and a screwdriver, and beyond that, a roll of duct tape.

It's genius, I think, maybe it's not genius. Maybe it's incredibly stupid. It doesn't matter. There's but seconds to spare before this place burns down and/or a demented killer pops out at me for a final confrontation. This is the strategy I'm going with. It's settled.

YEEP- YEEP – YEEP – YEEP

I lean my upper body onto the kitchen counter to keep my broken ankle from howling. It puts pressure on my chest. Every inhale feels like I'm getting stabbed by a knife made of my own bones. But I move, my left hand wraps its fingers as tight as possible around the butcher knife handle while the right winds it all up with duct tape.

I wrap until there's no duct tape left, and I have a scorpion tail for a left arm.

Whatever happens to me, whatever the final fight is, I will not drop my weapon. I will die with this blade in this palm.

—

With broken ribs, split lip, shattered teeth, a dripping hole in my hand, the other hand duct taped to a knife, and a, at the very least sprained ankle, I walk/crawl/limp out the back door and then around the house.

It's cold out. It smells like Christmas. The stars twinkle. It might be a nice night if I wasn't fighting for my goddam life.

It's kind of a dumb thought, but I catch myself thinking it; it will be nice if I survive this. God, I won't be cute for a very long time, I mean, I'll be messed up, sure. Not just physically, but mentally, I have no doubt that there will be months of recovery and probably years of therapy— I mean, I just set a dude on fire, *I saw his face melt off, I did that!* But—it will be nice to be alive if I get the chance to keep doing it.

A pizza sounds nice honestly; a big burned pizza with brown spots all over it. Really overdose that shit with the parmesan dust. Maybe a soda. Oh, and garlic knots. Christ, I hope I survive this, now I'm hungry too. Will I be able to eat with these split lips? Am I going to have to live on smoothies?

I take sloppy, limping steps through perfectly manicured blades of grass. Bleeding, coughing, hurting all over. It hurts just to breathe. I think a broken rib is now firmly planted into my lungs like the sword in the stone. I retch once, so hard that I feel a tooth come loose and fly out onto the lawn like an unpopped popcorn kernel.

Oh, I'm gonna have a hefty dentist bill if I make it through this, and the only dentist I know just got blown up by a car bomb.

I wander out to the front yard. The long, deep, sloped hill. All that's left now is to wait for the cops, and if the cops really can't make it in time, then it's up to me to stop The Rot-Mouth from leaving with Tommy.

When I reach the front yard, I find 7109 Chanticlair is a flaming terrarium. It's a lighthouse now. The harsh orange of the conflagration shines on the empty plots and the woods below the hill. It flows yellow and jumps red where the fire is hottest.

The glass front exposes the fury of the flame as it eats the drywall and carpet of the second floor. Sections of attic are on fire. Rich, auburn flames speckled with black dust and ribbons of confetti fabric. They cut through patches of roof so they can lick the night with smoke.

The first floor, with all its marble and hard stone, does not offer much for the fire to eat. But spots of the ceiling collapse. Fire runs down the walls and drops sections of framing. The chandelier above the dining room table comes crashing down and the crystals all scatter like cockroaches.

The wind blows through the house and toward me. It all stinks; that way fire stinks when it's eating chemicals and plastic.

A figure emerges within the glass house, out from the kitchen and into the living room; The Rot-Mouth. He carefully maneuvers a section of collapsed ceiling. He checks beneath the couch cushion; the place I was sitting when this whole mess got started.

I hide, meekly, behind a cube bush, right at the side of the van. A knife trembling in hand. The Rot-Mouth is on his way. He walks out from the house, maniacally coughing.

He removes his ski mask and I recognize him instantly. It's—it's Jeff Glazer.

He's not just alive—he's—here. He's in front of me. He *is* The Rot-Mouth. I'm so surprised that I forget to hide. I stand at the walkway's end, my head cocked like a curious dog.

An equally stunned Jeff Glazer leaves his house. His silhouette in flames as 7109 Chanticlair turns to ash and black fog in his wake. This is it, I think. That last part of the movie. The part where the babysitter either gets gutted or guts back. Nowhere to hide. Nowhere to run. I defiantly raise my blade/tapewad hand; I make the bravest stand I can make with one good foot.

"Hello, Narcissa," he says, so painfully casual.

I menace my duct-tape-butcher-knife arm, try to speak with my mouth transformed into three lips, "Thay back!"

He raises his hands. "I'm not gonna hurt you. It's okay."

"Don'thyou have a gun?" I ask him.

"No."

"Why?"

"I didn't think I'd need one," he admits.

To my surprise, once he's cleared from the house's perimeter, he simply drops. He sits down beside the stone walkway, legs spread far apart. He rubs his deodorant-soaked eyes. His jacket is open now, ever so slightly, revealing a bow tie and white tuxedo collar.

Behind him, the house combusts. The glass face of the Only House on Chanticlair Lane explodes, beads and shards and car-sized sheets of glass go tumbling into the front garden. It's a true dollhouse now, a home without a face, open to the night. Wind rushes inside to feed the fire. It takes to a grand piano, a couch. Liquor bottles explode in the bar.

I keep my knife ever ready, it shakes wildly. Any second now, I promise myself, any second, Jeff will pop back to a stand and he'll try to end things.

He looks up at me, so calmly. So completely unfazed by this whole nightmare. He points at his upper lip, the place where I got shot. "Did Chuck do that? Did he shoot you in the face?"

My blade trembles, my voice is only a blood soaked, hoarse whisper, "Yeah."

"What an idiot."

I realize it now; Chuck, better known as Charlie to me, was Charlie Glazer. I did babysit for him once, years and years ago; back when I was first starting out. I remember Charlie was a nervous man without hair. I think I went to him once for a teeth-cleaning. Does that count as irony? No? I'm not sure.

Jeff continues, his high-pitch rasp coming off as anything but threatening, "I know a good doctor. A plastic surgeon. He does cleft lip surgeries for babies. I bet he can make you look like new again."

"That's nice," blood and drool fall from my chin in a long gooey string.

A pause, punctuated with cackling fire.

"Whereth Thommy?" I ask him.

"The woods," He shakes his head, nods his head toward the tree-line surrounding the house. *At least I hope that's where he is.*

There's the sound of police sirens, now. The sound sneaks in from beneath the fire. I'm hesitant to take my eyes off Jeff. But, a faint turn of the head finds alternating red and blue flashes glowing through faraway fog drifts.

A section of housing collapses behind Jeff; the whole east wing sugar cube. Furniture of the guest and game room come crashing onto the lawn. A pool table scatters into a front yard tree, a bed flops face down beside it.

"How?" I ask Jeff, it's the only question I can think of to pass the time. "They thold me you got blowt up in a car bomb."

Jeff pulls on blades of grass with his fists; I've seen little boys do this when they're about to cry.

"We left a homeless guy who kinda looked like me in the driver's seat. Chuck was gonna fake the dental records down the line."

"But-but- but why?"

He shrugs. He clicks his tongue before he rolls it around his cheeks.

He explains to me, "'Cause it's hard."

"Whath-hard?"

He's so casual. He's so droll and unashamed it makes me just want to rush him and start stabbing until there isn't a face to stab anymore, but, I don't. I stand there, bleeding and broken limbed, and listen to this private island dentist whine.

"Oh, Narcissa—" he pauses to reflect. "This life. The wealth. The busy days. It seems easy but it's not. Everybody's always—they're always gnawing at you. Alouette's family, they were really quite insufferable. Didn't think I was good enough for her. Alouette herself, she had *expectations* that were hard to meet—but—this wasn't about her. I've spent my entire adult life in the mouths of other people. In their teeth and spit. And for what? For this house?"

He gazes back to 7109 Chanticlair. It burns. It screams.

"Tonight was about—starting over. At least it was supposed to be. I think I just wanted to go somewhere else. Be somebody else."

"Couldn't you have just gothen'a divorce? Or like gone part-thime, or bought a Porschth or thomething?"

"Yeah—" he trails off. "Yeah. *Maybe. Maybe.*"

He turns to his former home again, the fire is working its way to the back now. The kitchen cabinets are ablaze. Waterlines burst and the bottom floor is now host to a flood of steaming gray sewage. One has to hope the little boy got out, otherwise, by now, he's a well done cut of human veal.

The police are coming up the hill. I can see the strobe lights, I can hear the sirens. Must be the whole force and a firetruck to boot.

"I always hated this house," Jeff tells me. "Alouette wanted it. She wanted to be away from everybody. I always thought it was too cold. Look at it now; it's—it's too hot," he tells me, I think it might be a joke, he smiles ever so slightly. "To be honest with you; I'm happy to see it burn."

I seethe. A thick string of blood mixed with spit drips off my chin, thick like maple syrup,"You could'thave just moved thomewhere elth, you know."

He shakes his head at me, and laughs, once, one pitying bark of laughter. "You could never understand."

No, I really couldn't.

OLD MINT RIVER

I've been to a lot of NA meetings in my life.

A lot.

They're usually held in drab church basements or the back room of some decrepit office park, but here we are: an NA meeting under the stars and the blue cosmos; a flickering campfire at our heels.

The flames eat brush we collected ourselves. The smoke is bitter; it makes a dry smog that bites at my nose and stains my jacket with its stink.

There're five of us here, out in the middle of nowhere, North Georgia on the Appalachian Trail.

God help us. God help *me*. It's only the first night and my stomach hurts. I've got trail rash between my legs. My hands won't stop fucking shaking. Moments ago I had to shit in a hole for the first time in my life, and I'm not eager to continue doing that for the next month.

Jesus Christ—I'm not even totally dried out yet. My armpits are pumping buckets of ice water. I'm too hot. My skin feels chilly and prickly and loose. It's like I've got the flu, except this is a flu that yearns for cocaine.

—

This morning a van dumped us all off at a park and we just *went in*

—

Into the woods with nothing but tents and rain ponchos and shit trowels and boots. Canteens and meek provisions. We walked twelve grueling miles today. Over hills baking in the sun. All in the company of mosquitos.

Now, it's the close of the first day; the first of thirty obligatory NA meetings, and no one wants to talk. No one has hardly talked all day. It's been too hot. Too exhausting. We pop off our shoes and inspect our blisters. We wipe our grubby faces. We sweat and we chug water. Addicts, all of us, at one time or another.

The program director stands at a podium of fire. He's not as beat up as the rest of us. He's fifty years old, half of those sober. This is his program: *The Appalachian Rehabilitation*. Rolls off the tongue, I know. He does it four times a year and now he's got calves like a He-Man action figure. Our brutal trek was a mere walk in the park for him. Earlier, he introduced himself as *Counselor* Paul McAdams. I guess this is his summer camp.

McAdams is one of those half-caveman, half-college professor kinds of guys. He wears those billion pocket canvas pants and a maroon vest with trail patches. He's got long scraggly hair and an unkempt, round beard. His ugly face is like a harshly carved bar of soap; it's made doubly harsh by these outrageous blue smoke Elton John glasses.

"Alright, campers," he says in this smarmy, vegan-cheese-hippie yip.

I have to shake my head. He really just called us *campers*. I am *thirty-two years old*.

"Well, we all made it through our first day. Yeah! Yep-sir-ee! First day is always the toughest," he nods his head, and he's quiet, and he licks his lips like a preacher man. "Well, I'm sure you guys don't feel very good right now. In my fifteen years counseling at the Appalachian Rehabilitation, I haven't met one soul who was happy at the end of their first day— but you know what? I hope you're all proud of yourselves. You did it. You did the first '*it*' of many '*its*'. You put in the work and you got to the end of the day. Everybody here has got someone back home who's rooting for them and *wow-siree-bob*; you did it for them! Somewhere out there, under this same moon and these same stars, someone you love is going to bed tonight and, for the first time in a very long time, they're *not* worrying about you. They know you're finally on the trail to recovery."

There're four of us—*campers*; or rather, junkies from rich families. I assume this much as this whole Appalachian Trail rehab shit ain't cheap. I'll bet you Counselor McAdams has a nice mansion back in Atlanta if he's been doing this fifteen years. What a fucking con job it is. This operation has got to have zero overhead. No building. No guards. No employees— and I even had to buy my own goddam tent.

This isn't my first rehab. Let me tell you, I've been to some *choice* rehabs. Luxury resorts with spas and hot tubs and shit. I mean, the drying out sucks, it always sucks, but usually rehab is just a month at the spa. If you're lucky, there's maybe even a little tail. That's the fun part; thirteenth stepping with a piece of bleach blonde strange. I struggle to remember a time when I didn't find a rehab girlfriend for me to relapse with after we got out.

This, of course, is my first time in a men's only rehab. It's just dudes here; dudes shitting in holes and eating canned beans—four of us— *dudes*. We did a 'get-to-know-ya' game in the van to the drop-off point. Around the fire are Anesh, Oswald and Desmond.

Anesh: scrawny with a moptop. Innocent, black eyes like a lab rat. He's a West Coast kid, like me. Family owns an instant coffee company. I want to say he's a DJ or some other kind of bullshit musician that doesn't require the actual playing of instruments. Also like me, he's here for nose candy, but, from what I've gathered, a habit of synthetic marijuana has deep fried his brain into a golden brown hush puppy. Guy is a total space cadet.

Oswald: He's old. Like forty-five. He's got this wide-white-guy-frog face. A God-fearing Catholic who made a few mil as a crew manager with a family construction firm up in Michigan. He wears a big cross necklace and an orange-striped fishing shirt. He shattered his leg while skiing a few years back and got hooked on opiates. He turned himself in for rehab after he stole a bunch of money from his—*what was it*? I think it was his brother-in-law. He walks with a limp, and somehow this is the most interesting thing about him.

Finally, there's Desmond. Desmond is, like, twenty. Young, black kid with well-tended dreads and a screaming red t-shirt that's three sizes too big. His pants are hot pink, his shoes are thousand-buck white sneakers. Already ruined. A city boy. He's not made for the woods. He's too clean. Desmond hasn't shared anything about himself. He's quiet. A mean, stewing, quiet—but, so long as we're guessing; I read him as one of those kids who likes to dress and talk like he's from the wrong side of the tracks, but, seeing as he's here, I'd guess he's never missed a Christmas; he probably got busted melting heroin in a silver spoon.

"Tanner," Counselor Fuckhead McCheese says my name, "How about you start us off?"

"Me?" My voice trembles, my hands tremble too. "I-I-I don't have anything to say."

"Nothing?"

"Yeah. Nothing."

"You don't have anything on your mind?"

"No."

"Well, how about your heart—*how do you feel*?"

"Not great."

The counselor wisens his eyes, I'm playing right into his trap. "Why not?"

"I guess—" I pause, there're eight eyeballs on me in a flickering firelight. "I-I guess I'm embarrassed that I'm here."

"So, you feel shame?" He takes a sip from a sticker-bombed canteen. "You want to talk about it? Go ahead. Introduce yourself to the group; just talk from the heart."

I find myself gripping my wrist. "Okay, uh, my name is Tanner Jaffe, but, uh, yeah," I sniffle, "—and, well, I guess it's kind of obvious, but, yeah, I'm uh—I'm an addict."

They do the thing you've seen on TV. They say *'hi Tanner'* in this muttered church choir.

"Uh. My last bump was Tuesday morning. I cleaned out the supply before the van came for me—uh, what else can I say? What do you want me to say? Uh—er—uh—There is a demon that lives inside of me, he has no name, but he, uh, this demon, he, uh, makes me do coke. And when there is no coke to be had, he makes me do crazy things to get it—and if I do enough coke, I become the demon and I do demonic kinds of things. How is that, counselor? Is that what I'm supposed to say?"

I say all of this deadpan. Lifeless and insincere. The eyeballs stare. No one provides comment. I don't think they're even allowed to respond. I'm on stage. This is slam poetry, this is free verse rap. I hate it.

I can't stand the silence, so I fill it up. "Uh. I took my first bump when I was seventeen. Yeah. Spring break in Amsterdam. Snuck away with some cousins. It was, um, love at first snort. What else— can I—uh—say? My family is quite wealthy, so, uh, it's never been too hard to acquire coke. Uh—my dad, uh, in the 70s and 80s he owned a textile company that made discount tuxedos, you know, easily tailored rentals for proms and weddings, but, uh, he's more famous now as a candidate for the California Senate. You know; *Steve Jaffee*; Proposition Triple-One. The, uh, *pray the gay away guy.* Yeah, that's my—old man. He, uh, asked me to attend this, er, *sobriety workshop* as a last ditch effort to get me on the right track and —uh, here I am I guess—sorry, I'm-I'm not so good at this."

"You said you were feeling shame," McAdams taunts me, "Let's break that down."

"*Well-uh-ackch-* I mean isn't this all supposed to make me feel ashamed? This is a punishment, right? I mean, sure we can use the words *therapy* and *rehab* and *camp* as much as we want, but, uhhh, this *is* a punishment. We're all here because we're too rich for prison, but we've done bad things and our families are sick of our shit. So—yeah. I think this whole *'boy scouts wandering in the woods'* thing is designed to make me feel punished and embarrassed. Maybe even hurt a little bit. I mean, maybe I *should* be ashamed—we should all be ashamed. I mean, I should be home right now, with my family. I should be working, uh, a decent job and doing tai-chi every morning at six A.M. But instead I'm here in, uh, buttfuck, Appalachia; talking about my feelings over cans of beans and twig smoke."

McAdams chuckles, "Buddyboy, you got twenty-nine more nights out here in *Buttfuck* Appalachia. You better get used to talking about your feelings."

It bothers me, the way he says *fuck*. It's the way a judge or a preacher would say it. He hates that word but he's throwing it back at me as if to tell me that the cussin' won't scare him off.

I lick my lips, "Okay, then, so how about you tell me, Counselor: what do you want me to say?"

"I'm not your screenwriter, brother. I'm not your puppet master either. I'm nothing but a pair of ears. So, you've told us that this is a punishment; well, Tanner, if that's the case, what are you being punished for?"

The other campers observe me. Titillated. These poor souls have been fighting mud, trees and hills all day. I'm their television now and they want some entertainment.

I pause, I watch my fingers lock and unlock. "I guess—I'm at the end of a long line of things I need to be punished for. I've always been a fuck up. I've *always* had trouble with coke. It's no secret. The whole state of California knows how much I love coke. It's on CBC two times a week —Uh—Coke is like—" I close my eyes, it's easier this way. "I-I-I mean, I've never understood how people got addicted to other drugs. Alcohol? Forget it, take a nap. Hallucinogens, leave them for the tree-huggers. Meth, it's like putting your head in a microwave, but, coke is like—Do you guys know how they make coke? Any of you? Have any of you ever seen a thing about it on the Edu-TV? *How It's Made*? Cocaine is a leaf, first obviously, but they soak the leaves in gasoline. Yeah, pure, uh, unfiltered gasoline. That's what makes it into a powder; that's what gives it its distinct chemical flavor. So—coke is not a drug, really, it is fuel concentrate. You put it into your brain and you feel like a monster truck, like an airplane; a fucking stealth bomber. You feel like your hypothalamus has got eight cylinders of raw diesel power. And the best part is, you don't feel crazy. Not at the moment. You just feel powerful and happy and fast—Coke is all of the drugs, it's the whole drug rainbow—it's all the good feelings—and it makes the world make sense—so—yeah—I love coke—I adore coke—and I've done a lot of bad things for coke. And I've embarrassed my dad a lot so—you know—"

I trail off. With eyes shut I am alone in darkness.

"In 2016 my dad read the writing on the wall and transitioned from a life in business to one in politics. You, knowing following a *certain someone's* footsteps. And now he's a family values senator, trying to flip California red— so, he's got a tough job ahead of him and it's hard enough to be a black republican in this country, but it only makes it harder when his son is out wrapping Lambo's around light posts or getting busted with, uh, *crack-whores* to use a—er, politically insensitive term."

I open my eyes. Nothing has changed. There is still fire. Four men around it.

"After my last car accident, he requested that I get sober for him. And I did it. You know, I really did it. I went to a nice facility with swimming pools and yoga and shit—and I, uh, started 2017 as a clean man —and so—you know—as part of staying that way, my dad thought that I needed a carrot on a stick to stay away from my worst impulses, so, he told me he would help me start a business. Any business I wanted. So, I told him I was going to start a restaurant, a, er, steakhouse. Uh, we have a friend of the family who is a professional chef. You guys know, uh, Coastside Farms? Watson Steak Company? *Wicked Ambition*, the band? Yeah, Jack Watson is a personal friend of the family. My dad's office is full of his signed guitars; we grew up going to his concerts for free, backstage passes and all that. You know, it's no secret, Jack Watson struggled with addiction too. So, he got it. He understood my addiction. So you know, he kinda kept an eye on me, like a sponsor, uh, I guess, but we were business partners too; so—"

I've lost track. I must sound like a deranged lunatic. My ear suddenly itches, I scratch it wildly—

"So—me and Jack Watson, we're business partners, starting a restaurant. That's all that matters. So, yeah, for the first time in my life, I was doing real work. Like, I was making spreadsheets and I was researching properties and, you know, hiring the kids who were gonna wash our dishes. We ended up buying a building on the Sunset Strip, and I got this sort-of girlfriend who was going to be the restaurant's social media and hype manager. It was actually kind of cool; it was gonna be like a high end Hard Rock Café, you know, like Hard Rock Café but classy and with ninety dollar plates—and I invented this— this concept of personalized experience dinners where you could, like, pay to dine out with rockstars and stuff, you know, the ultimate superfan dining experiences—acoustic shows—and… and, uh….it was all—you know it was all pretty kick-ass—and I don't know—I guess—right before the restaurant opened—I got too excited and I fell into some old habits."

The fire cackles. Crickets sing. Counselor McAdams leans in—he smells where this story is going.

"It only took one bump—I was at a meeting with some potential investors and they brought some coke out— and I thought I could take it—but then, one bump was one bender, and then— I, uh, I guess I became *the demon*—as I've put it. I—ended up selling our kitchen equipment to make way for a second bender and—I—well—when my dad confronted me about it I—uh—tried to stab him? Just a little bit?"

It leaves my mouth in the form of a question, but there's no doubt that it's what I did.

"I was out of my mind. You know. Coke rage. The world is a beautiful place when you're on cocaine, but when you're coming down, you get— angry— that you're coming down. I was mad at my father. And he was rightfully mad at me. We were at his house. My parents' house and — he told me he was going to send me—well—to this thing; to a men's only survivalist camp in the Georgia wilderness, and I—uh—went after him with a letter opener. I never, uh, actually put a knife *into* him. I should clarify. I just kinda, I—stabbed and slashed *at* him. I worked him into a corner. My step-mom came home from Pilates, you know, thank God, right at the right time, and she threw a lamp at me— it was a whole *thing*—anyways—my dad wasn't about to let the papers know what happened so, now, I'm, *uh*, here, uh, here with all you lovely guys."

McAdams soaks in my story; he sits there like a big wheel of Vermont cheddar cheese, just stinking with psychology 101 fun facts. He is at the ready with a question, it pops out of him. "Would you say that your relationship with drugs is intertwined with a relationship with violence?"

I dodge the question, I can see the other campers are salivating.

"—I should clarify, everybody here signed an NDA, right? If just one of these stories leak to the press my dad will sue everyone here into the stone age."

"No one's gonna leak your stories, Tanner. We might have come here as individuals, as broken, lonely people, but when we emerge thirty days from now, we will emerge as a team. By the end of our journey, the five of us won't have any secrets."

"Yes, I get all that about the journey, but they *did* sign the NDAs, yeah?"

"Yes. Yes they did. Your father's secretary made sure."

—

Counselor McCheesewheel asks me some questions about drugs. And how drugs make me feel. And how drugs make me act. This isn't my first rodeo. This is, in fact, my ten thousandth rodeo. The questions all blend together and eventually we get into the territory of repetition. Then the spotlight moves away from me.

You do enough of this rehab stuff and other people's speeches start to feel familiar. They might have new faces, new voices, but stories like the ones told by Anesh and Oswald and McAdams are basically reruns for me.

Anesh doesn't have a brain; like I suspected. He fell off the old skateboard one too many times. His head is void of any thoughts and so it was easy to fill it up with every substance known to man. He grew up with immigrant parents. They had no idea what was going on and no idea how to discipline him. He talks about missing his grandmother's funeral and a week he spent in the looney bin. It's all quite sad; but it's all quite boring too.

Oswald is a cryer. He bawls into his hands and talks about Jesus and occasionally stares up at the stars, with snot trailing down his chin and will say something like, *God forgive me for what I have done.* The guy stole eight hundred dollars from his brother-in-law to get some illegal downers. It's honestly not that bad.

Counselor McCheesewheel takes a turn himself. He's had twenty years of NA to perfect his monologue. It's all so theatrical. He soliloquizes like Patrick Stewart delivering Macbeth. If you strip away the pulp, it's not a particularly interesting tale. He was once a fucklehead crank on the streets of Albuquerque. High on methamphetamine and drunk off his ass, he found himself behind the wheel of a large (stolen) automobile and flattened a jaywalking rich girl at a crosswalk: an heiress to a magazine company of all people. He served his time. Got a degree in psychology while he was still in his orange jumpsuit. And here he is now: making millions of dollars to go camping. He can say all he wants to say about shame, but I'll bet you, deep down, running over that girl was the best thing that ever happened to his net worth.

Finally, the circle reaches its last participant, Desmond. He sits furthest from the fire, dreadlocks and pink pants cast in shadows. He scowls like he was hoping the counselor would conveniently forget him.

Cheesewheel says his name, "Desmond, you're up."

"I got nothing to say."

"I'm afraid it doesn't work that way, Buckaroo. Everybody here said their piece. What's yours?"

He bites his lower lip, "I don't have a story."

The counselor chuckles, "Everybody's got a story."

He shrugs, "Not me."

There's a lengthy silence. Our eyes move back and forth from Cheesewheel to Desmond as they enter into a stand-off of wills.

"I can't make you talk, Desmond."

"Good—then don't."

"Is that really the attitude you want to bring to the circle? To the team? You want to be this team's dead weight?"

"__"

"Okay," Cheesewheel concedes. "Nobody can make you speak your truth. This isn't torture. What I will tell you is this: you're not the first guy on this trail who thought he was too good for it. This trail will break you, Desmond. It's a long way to West Virginia. If the woods don't break you, then maybe it will be the mountains or the rain or the bugs. So, you better prepare yourself. The more you fight it, the more you are gonna feel it. Feelings are powerful creatures. They'll sneak up, bite you right in the face."

"Man, fuck you."

Cheesewheel laughs out the nose. He's heard this before too.

—

It astounds me, but the night just keeps getting darker, and the crickets just keep getting louder. We sit around for an entire hour, doing jack shit. Mending our backpacks. Drinking water. Brushing our teeth. Cheesewheel encourages us to speak amongst ourselves, but no one wants to. No one but Oswald, anyway, he only wants to cry on his counselor's shoulder.

Eventually, it's bedtime, or seeing as there aren't beds, maybe it's *bagtime.*

Five campers retire to their tents. Thank God we get our own tents, right? If I had to spend my nights huffing one of these freaks sleep-farts, I would choke myself to death with my own hands.

Yeah, the solitude of this nylon bag will no doubt become the sad highlight of this trip.

We've got forty-five minutes until lights out. We're encouraged to journal in this time. Or read. There's only so much room in my backpack though. Most of it is reserved for dehydrated food and life straws and spare socks, but, praise Jesus, I saved some room for a calico-patterned notebook and a fresh copy of *Addicted to Addiction* by Dr. Dabney Endicott. Cheesewheel himself was kind enough to gift it to me. I poked through it in the van to the drop-off point. Lots of steps. Lots of Venn diagrams and pretty metaphors.

I try to read, but this book feels like it was written by an over-eager tenth grader who has still kept their DARE promise. Plus it's too quiet. I can hear Oswald crying—and if I'm not mistaken—I think I hear Anesh jacking off.

This rehab sucks. What I wouldn't give for some headphones. Or a memory foam pillow. Or a manic pixie rehab bunny. Or an Xbox. Or a hot meal. Or just some air conditioning. Hell, at this point I'd pay something like 10,000 dollars for just a white noise machine and a stack of cardboard boxes to put under this tent.

I try to sleep. Best I can. And if I can't sleep I'll just shut my eyes and be thankful I'm not walking.

—

I guess you don't know how luxurious a toilet is until you don't have one.

Even guys in prison have a toilet. It's a foot from their damn bed.

I wake up in the middle of the night and I need to piss, but, getting up to piss is a whole process. So, I hold it. I nearly piss my sleeping bag. I wake up again and I need to piss so bad it physically hurts. But still, I don't want to go through with the whole getting up process. Eventually it's three A.M. and I feel like piss might come out of my ears.

So, I wake up. I unpack myself from my bag and get on my shirt, boots and grab my flashlight.

It's dark outside. The moon is small and meaningless, obscured by branches. *Fuck you, moon.*

Maybe if you grow up with this shit you get used to it, but I think the darkest place I've ever been is a movie theater. I shine my flashlight out from our clearing and into the branches of an ocean of trees. Suddenly my head is flooding with every movie jump-scare I've seen in the last ten years. My peripheral vision is filled with little Linda Blairs with white eyes and green scab faces. I keep expecting something to pop out and shriek at me.

I go to the woods and carefully shine my light through a maze of twigs, scanning for ghouls, goblins, ghosts, whatever else.

When I decide the coast is clear, I let it all out and piss on a branch.

"Hey,"

A voice is calm and casual, but I'm so on edge I almost swing around and piss on whoever is behind me.

"You scared the fuck out of me—Jesus—*Fuck you*, dude."

It's Desmond. At least I think it is. All I see are two white spots for eyes hidden in what appear to be his dreads. I put my cock away.

"What, you need something?" I ask him, I shine my light at his feet.

He hesitates and bites his lower lip. God, I hope this isn't a sex thing. There's twenty-nine more days of this nature hike with this kid. I will have zero desire to get sober if I have to come home with sexual trauma.

"*Rich kid—Rich kid,*" Desmond mocks me. "I've been trying to catch a word with you."

I see a smile crack. Oh, it's *not* a sex thing. It's a meal ticket thing. I readjust my flashlight and can clearly see dollar bills rolling where his pupils used to be. I should have seen this coming. I'm not a stranger to punks trying to chisel a few bucks out of me. I wonder, what will it be this time, blackmail? A threat of violence?

"So, this is an ambush." I puff my chest. "What do you want from me?"

He shows me his palms. "I come in peace."

"Yeah. Sneaking up on me in the middle of the night. Real peaceful. You got something to sell me, go ahead, sell it."

He doesn't miss a beat. "You're a cokehead, yeah? Tell me this, rich kid, what would you do for a gram right now?"

I don't miss a beat either. "I'd shoot a golden retriever puppy in the skull. I'd—take a piss on my grandma's face, what do you want me to say? I'd do anything. *Fuck you*, what, did you smuggle in a crack rock? Think I'm gonna trade you all my freeze-dried scrambled eggs for an ounce of drywall?"

He shrugs and purses his lips. "Hey, if you're not interested—"

"Sorry—" I hold a hand near my temple. "It's been a long day. What do you got?"

"Nothing on me," he checks over his shoulder for the campsite, then returns at a lower volume. "Just a rumor."

"Yeah, about what?"

He flashes his light out into the woods.

"It's a long trail," Desmond waxes poetic. "Runs more than 2000 miles. All the way to Maine. Lots of empty spaces. One could, theoretically, run a whole criminal enterprise somewhere out here. Probably never get caught."

"Whatever it is you've got to say, you should say it."

"You ever heard of the Old Mint River?" Desmond cuts to the chase.

"Can't say that I have."

"At the start of the nineties, when the Coast Guard got a real hard-on for drugs coming into the ports and just about every dealer, importer, and drug lord was going to prison, there was an effort by some young entrepreneurs to take the cocaine business domestic," he rubs his mustache stubble. "There's a farm out here. A coca leaf farm out in the middle of nowhere. Runs premium shit out of Minton's Pass to PCB, B-More and New York on roads where nobody thinks to look. Some folks call it the Old Mint River."

I find the story dubious. "They grow coca leaves? Here? Appalachia? What, in an underground cave?"

"No. A little farm, like I said, in the open sunshine. Hey, if there's a dollar to be made, somebody is gonna make it— maybe it's not something you understand—but your *dad* certainly does."

Alarm bells are going off in the sections of my brain that still function properly. Everything about this sounds like bullshit. In all likelihood, this is a scheme to get me kidnapped or murdered or arrested. The best-case scenario is that Cheesewheel put him up to this as a means to test my commitment to sobriety, but even this is farfetched. I should tell this kid to *fuck off*, but—other, larger sections of my brain are still ruled by the Incan god of Cocoiana and his warlord spirit sometimes makes decisions for me.

—So, I bite. "Alright, you've got your history lesson, what's your pitch?"

"Seventeen days from now. Tennessee. Two of us take a detour. I got a map. I got some extra supplies. We'll meet up with some *friends of mine* on Minton's Pass. They can hook you up with uncut, farm-to-nose, purest cocaine this side of the equator. *Made In America*."

I guess they call it fiending because it really does feel like there's a fiend inside of me. There's a gnarly little gremlin, he's in my stomach and my heart. I feel him swinging between my ribs like they're monkey bars. I guess I'm just a fool for advertising, but I imagine clean coke; real snow-blizzard, bleach-white, whole-milk shit, and at just the thought of it, I get a chub, and I cry a little, and I start to salivate. I even sniffle, on pure instinct. I have to take a hard breath.

"Interesting," I play it cool. "Very interesting. I'm sure there would be an astronomically high price for something like that?"

"This isn't about money—not immediately anyways," he laughs. "Maybe it is about money in the long run—but not where you're concerned."

I swallow. I sniffle. My hands shake.

He continues, "Friends of mine are looking to make some friends in high places. You went to business school, yeah, Rich Kid? So, you know how it is; it's all about who you know."

It takes me about five seconds to do the math. Desmond isn't actually in rehab. He's here for me. He's here for my name. He's a goddamned sleeper agent.

"Is this about my dad?" I put the last pieces together. "My dad doesn't play dirty, dude. Maybe if you sold guns or, uh, ran a gay-to-straight conversion camp, he'd go for a sit down, but if your people think they're gonna buy me off with coke and then have your confederate cartel get buddy-buddy with my dad, you're—you're bananas in pajamas, man. He'd squeal so fast to the DEA they'd probably carpet bomb the whole Appalachian trail."

"It's not like that—"

"So, what is it like? Enlighten me."

"These friends of friends of mine have some legitimate investments in the tobacco industry. The way we see it: long term strategy, your dad is, let's just say he's *old school cool.* One of those *bring back the old ways* kind of guys—"

I stare. Void of thought.

"Maybe he'd agree with us when we say that the culture war on cigarettes has gone too far. We think it'd be nice to see smoking allowed again in airports and college campuses. Maybe even get smoking back in the movies. It's a free country, right?"

Now I'm the one chuckling.

He continues. "Don't think too hard about the big picture. Here's the headline for you: on day seventeen of this program, you come with me for a detour. We meet some friends on the Old Mint River, and they get you your first snort of a lifetime supply of the best coke in the U.S. In exchange; we get an audience with California's next republican Senator."

"So—what then? You're gonna blackmail my dad into passing legislation that reduces smoking bans in public places? And that's only if he wins, which, let's be clear, is still-a-million to one long-shot. That's the —uh, big picture I don't need to think too hard about? That's a hell of a plan, Desmond. Who came up with it, Rube Goldberg?"

"It doesn't have to be blackmail. And he doesn't have to win—all that's to say: story's got the same ending no matter what," he holds out his hand to make a deal. "You get coke, big tobacco makes a new friend. A *mean* friend."

I take a long pause and I try to think hard about this, but it's funny, sometimes I try to think hard, and my brain is like an engine that just won't start. Without coke, I'm dry. I'm empty. My thoughts sputter and smoke and do not move. I have no cognitive momentum. I try to think about the deal, the implications, but, really, I just stand there, looking at some guy's palm. I really don't think much at all.

"Day seventeen, you said?"

He nods.

"Let me—" I can't believe the words coming out of my mouth. "Let me try to get sober for a few days. I'll let you know if I flunk out."

His hand retreats. We head back to our tents.

—

One day turns to two days. Which then turns to three days. Three turns to five. Five days turn into ten. We put in the miles. O'er woods and mountains we go. Georgia turns to North Carolina as we approach the Tennessee panhandle. Of course, it's all the same in the woods: rocks and canopies and mosquitos. Dirt. Dirt. Dirt. My feet turn into purple yams. The inside of my calves turn into salmon fish scales.

No one makes much small talk. No one wants to. We eat canned goods. We climb mountains of yellow bush. We run blisters into our heels when someone sees a snake. This is what the Vietnam War felt like, I often think, lugging backpacks through a forest that wants to kill us, only instead of firefights with the Vietcong we have nightly NA meetings, which are worse, honestly. Most nights I wish a little Vietnamese soldier would put a bullet in my head. It would be easier than listening to the Cheesewheel drag on about self-help books. And listening to Oscar welp and cry to Jesus or Anesh umming and erring his way through fifteen minutes of K2-diminished show-and-tell.

Through all of this, Desmond never opens up. Not once. And why should he? He's a fraud. He's not even a real addict. Every night the Cheesewheel asks him his story and Desmond tells him to fuck right off and Cheesewheel gives him fifteen minutes of NA prophecy.

I wish I had gone with his strategy. I have to deliver slam poetry every night.

—

Ten days turns to eleven. Somehow. The further we go, the longer these days seem to get.

Shitting in the woods, I find, is not pleasant— and walking in on Counselor Cheesewheel shitting in the woods is doubly unpleasant. This happens on the evening of the eleventh day. I turn a corner and there's his hairy college-professor ass. He turns back with grit teeth. He says. "*Uh, oh, occupado!*" as I watch a yellow turd fall out of his ass. Disgusting. I am too rich to witness such an atrocity.

The trail is hot and sticky, and my body becomes a minefield of different rashes and blisters and bug bites. Supplies run low and one day we fish for our dinner out of a river. Another night we eat wild huckleberries. These activities are supposed to encourage a sense of wellness, but nothing, and I mean *nothing,* has ever made me jones harder for cocaine than foraging for food.

—

The twelfth night. Cheesewheel McAdams tells us that we hike the Appalachian trail because it's the second hardest trail in the United States, and the first hardest trail, he tells us, is the twelve steps to sobriety. Cue your eye rolls. *Sobriety is a lonely trek through hostile woods,* he says. *It's a journey over mountains of self-doubt and through the riptides of rivers of temptation. It's an expression of perseverance. We became addicts because we were weak, we become sober because we are strong.*

He's like a fucking human fortune cookie.

It all gets old. So much of NA is just poetry. It's this song and dance of similes and metaphors that try to make the emptiness, and the hunger, feel brave. Feel meaningful. But it isn't brave. It isn't meaningful. It's just hunger. It's a dull pang for drugs. You can throw as much color as you want at it, the brew is always black.

I get up to talk at the nightly NA meeting and it is expected of me to scramble together my shame and my worst impulses into some kind of dragon to slay— or epic quest to be undertaken. But it's not really like that. Addiction isn't a real enemy and sobriety isn't a real destination. I am going nowhere. We are all going nowhere. We have no monsters to kill. It's all empty, like the darkness itself.

Cheesewheel speaks; he says life is cast in darkness. He tells us that to live is to walk in a shadow of night. He tells us that there are candles we carry through life. For some of us the candle is family, for others it is religion. For others it may be a career or a hobby. Some of us have many candles. Some of us have but one— But, to survive, he says, to make something out of this life, we must find a light that guides us— And all I can think as he spins this endless metaphor is how bright a candle can be made with *drugs*. Cocaine specifically. If family and exercise and waking up at six A.M are candles, then cocaine is surely one of those flashlights that can set fire to a piece of paper. It's Agent Orange. It's TNT.

I miss coke.

I say this in my session, that twelfth night, and I say this to myself when I hike the endless trail. I miss coke the way a starving-to-death babe misses its mother's tit. I miss coke the way an angry ghost misses the body taken from it. Try my best, there are no poems for it. There are no metaphors that capture the feeling. The nightly poetry falls through my hands and when I go to bed, I dream about snorting lines and the way it made my snot drip taste like a lawnmower.

—

We hike when the sun rises. Most mornings Cheesewheel will play taps on an MP3 speaker and us addicts will shuffle out of our tents and slog our blisters into the twiggy branches and the first purple light of day.

Sometimes, slogging my backpack on another back trail, I'll catch a plane running overhead and I'll imagine jumping so high that I land on the wing —and I ride the plane to wherever the fuck it's going, and I go to the worst neighborhood in that city and hound the streets for crack.

Desmond's offer is never far from my mind, our prospective detour on the seventeenth night; Old Mint River and the promise of cocaine fit for Zeus. I think I'll do it some days. Other days I don't. I never show Desmond my cards though. I never let him know.

I don't want to get sober. Not really. But I don't want to do cocaine anymore either. I don't have the right metaphor to describe the feeling, but, I want to try on sobriety. I want to sample it. I want to see if it fits. A part of me thinks of coming home on day thirty, and maybe it will feel nice to be clean for a little while; to plunge into the darkness, with open, pawing hands searching for new candles.

—

It rains on the seventeenth day. A summer monsoon as we climb a trail called Devil's Whip into Tennessee. Water falls like bullets; they bounce off the hood of my rubber slicker. We hike straight upward into the storm clouds themselves— mountain climbing through mud.

Oscar is the first to fall. He plops down and the shit cakes into his fingers and knees. I think we all have a laugh, but by the end of the second hour we've all fallen down. We're all caked in mud; it's on our faces, it's in our asscracks and between our toes. We climb higher and higher, until the plants die away and we're on our hands and knees pulling through rocks and thin air.

I don't know what time it is when it finally stops, but, eventually, the last bullet falls. We come across a clearing of boulders and without prompt we all sit down to catch our breath.

Usually, after a particularly hard section of trail, Cheesewheel will give us some bullshit lauding about our efforts, but, I think even he's had too much shit beaten out of him. We all find our spots far away from one another and bask in the simple pleasure of a sky that's not dunking rain.

I must fall asleep for a few minutes, but when I wake up there's someone standing over me.

It's Desmond.

He's absolutely wrecked from the trail. His rain poncho hardly fits him. His once pristine dreadlocks hang over his face like seaweed. Holes have worn into his pants. His shoes are wrecked. He's got rings under his eyes, black and purple and ash. He looks like a corpse that's just washed up on the shore from an angry river. I'm sure I do too.

"Tonight's the night," He mutters, voice broken, voice weak. "It's decision time, Rich Kid."

Desmond has been bothering me a lot the last few days. He's been sneaking up next to me during a piss or when we were both at the back of the pack. He'll ask where my head is at. I usually just tell him I haven't made a decision yet. But I suppose time has run out on that answer.

After what we just went through, I almost feel like I should try to stay sober out of pure martyrdom. Besides, with all this sweating, I'm cleaned out. That fiend, that coke goblin in my guts, he's begun to starve to death. I can feel him, laid out on my intestines as if they were a gurney. That demon in me, he breathes heavy and ragged. Maybe I—*I don't know*—Maybe I'll be alright without coke. Maybe I'll start going to the gym or get really into organic foods.

I tell Desmond as much. "I don't think it's gonna happen, man."

He's careful to make sure Cheesewheel isn't in earshot. "No?"

"No."

"Can I ask why?"

"'Cause… *fuck*…Maybe I'm gonna get clean."

Desmond is not so good at hiding his disappointment. "Yeah? Yeah, that's great for you. Happy for you, man."

"Let me ask you something, Desmond, 'cause I've been curious about this. Did they put you in here just for me? Your friends? Are they paying you to go through this rehab trail?"

He doesn't answer.

"How much did they pay you? You get a commission? 'Cause this shit sucks, but at least I came here for something. I can't imagine doing this for—for pretend."

"Look, man; you want to talk about what's real and what's pretend? The people I work for, they're some real mother fuckers. They got hands in everything; Hollywood Hills, Capital Hill. It's not just cigarettes and coke. You don't want to come with me on the detour for a high, fine, come with me tonight for your future."

"How do you mean?"

"*Your future.* Your legacy or whatever. You've said it yourself. You're a fuck up. The whole country sees you as a fuck up. You're the punch-line druggie son of America's foremost Uncle Tom— Come with me tonight. Come meet *my people.* If it's not coke you want, they'll cut another deal."

My mouth falls open into a grin, but I don't say anything.

He asks. "What do you want, a career? You want a celebrity girlfriend? You want to make movies? We can—"

"I think I want to get sober, Desmond."

"Aight," he sighs, deeply. "I didn't want it to come to this—but—"

After another careful glance to make sure the other campers are sleeping, or eating, or otherwise indisposed, Desmond reaches into a particular pocket. I know what he's grabbing long before he grabs it.

Obscured from eavesdroppers, he flashes a little white bag at his chest. A dime of sugar. And the man wasn't lying. Shit is white. If it really is coke and not baby laxative, this guy has some pure-as-pure-gets coke. The sick fiend in my guts falls out of his gurney. He tries to crawl out of my asshole so he can snort it himself.

"C'mon man, that's not—that's not cool."

Desmond slides the baggie into the pocket of my rain poncho. I'm too tired to stop him, or maybe I don't want him to stop.

"You want to get sober. Pour it out."

—

It doesn't rain any more. Still plenty of mud to trudge through, but no more rain. We crest the mountain and begin our descent from Devil's Whip.

Coming down a mountain sounds so easy, but then you do it, and it just sucks in a different way from climbing up. It's easier to fall; you have to bend your ankles in these funky positions. I wonder if there's a metaphor here for building a life after rehab.

The coke burns a hole in my pocket these last few miles. It'd be so easy, I think. Sneak off for a piss, take a snort. It's no different than any dinner party. The fiend does jumping jacks around my guts. He howls like a kindergartener for a Happy Meal. He says we can make the bag last a week, in little doses. He claims we could even make it last the rest of the trek if we use it sparingly, but I think both of us know that wouldn't happen.

—

Darkness comes, as it always does.

The storm delayed us; Cheesewheel wanted to get us to a recreational spot at the bottom of the mountain where there are showers and even a food store, but we simply don't have the time or energy.

We build camp tonight in the heart of some heavy woods; hardly even a clearing. Our tents are constructed between the jail-bars of tree trunks. We construct our fire in the least *tree-y* spot we can find, and here we set up our sitting blankets, our mini chairs.

Some of us dry our clothes on the fire. Others simply hold out clammy hands. Others eagerly eat cold beans or granola. The fire snaps. It's quiet. The smoke is choked with wet brush and rises in foul-smelling, white-steam. We stink too, I'm sure, Oscar in particular. Old guy must have shit his pants.

I don't think anyone feels up for a session, but Counselor Cheesewheel McAdams calls for it anyway. Ragged and soaked, with his hair like a rat's nest, he stands before us with this hideous church pastor flavor of side smile. I can see it in his horn-rimmed glasses; he's cooking up some fresh metaphors for us.

"Devil's Whip trail, huh? If ever there was a more appropriate name. Now: *If the beginning is the hardest part*," he says, he raises a finger, "—*And the ending is the hardest part, then surely, the middle is the hardest part too*. That's one of my favorite quotes from Doctor Dabney Endicott from his work: *Sobriety for the Western Soul*. Gentlemen, tonight we raise our water canteens to what was surely the hardest part of our journey. One of many hardest parts, am I right?"

The junkies grumble in affirmation. Oscar and Anesh raise their canteens. Desmond and I do not.

"We might have climbed a mountain, but today's trek was our journey through the Valley of Death. Now, I know everybody here is tired. Everybody here is beat up. I'm sure every one of you could say there was a point on today's hike when you said to yourself, *I can't do this. I want to give up.* But look around you. You made it. *We all made it.* Nine miles in the pouring rain, straight upward over the hostile trails of Mount Eustace. Yes, gentlemen, your feet are blistered, your legs are weary, I'm sure your very souls are soaking wet, but, hey, you made it. You—made—it! Say it to yourself, say it with me. I made it. *I made it.* And if you made it here, if you made it over this mountain and through this day, surely you can make it when you get back home."

He's really earning that paycheck.

"We should rest. We have another long day ahead of us tomorrow —but first—I think we should go around the circle. Tanner, how about you lead us off?"

"Me?" I take a sip of water and shrug, this many days in, I've learned I can't just say that I've got nothing to say. He'll just badger me; no, it all moves faster if I just bullshit out a sad story or a rhyme about recovery.

So I speak, not from the heart, no, but, with my tongue. "Well, as of this morning, I've been sober from narcotics for seventeen days. Which is a lot. It's a lot more than I thought I could do and— Yeah, today, sucked and—"

Jesus, what is there to even talk about? I've given these people everything at this point from how I lost my virginity to my week in jail to painstakingly vivid details of my father's worst megalomaniacal meltdowns. I consult the circle, four faces disfigured by the trail are glowing in red, yellow and black shadow. Desmond gives me daggers.

"Today I really wanted to break. I'm used to three star restaurants and after hours clubs—the occasional helicopter ride—so hiking through the sticks, on Devil's Whip, with shit on my knees and ice water in my socks—it made me feel like I was in the depths of hell itself. And— Counselor, you talk like we're supposed to feel proud. But I don't feel proud. I feel angry. I feel angry and, now, more than ever, more than ever before in my whole life, I want to get high."

Cheesewheel leans back and clasps his nose with either of his pointer fingers. "Go on."

"That's it. That's all there is to it. If there was an escape pod. If I could push a button and make this all go away. I would push it. And drugs are a damn good escape pod."

"So you want to get high? I understand that. A part of you will always want to get high, Tanner. That's our disease. Me? I've been sober twenty years—"

—Any excuse to remind us—

"—I want to get high too," he says. "Right now. I do. I always will. So—let's rephrase our terms here, Tanner. You want to get high, so what? Here's the real question, buckaroo, do you still want to get sober? Because, this trip will be over in thirteen little days, then a few weeks in outpatient, and then, the only thing keeping you from diving headfirst back into addiction is Y-O-U. So, think about this before you answer, maybe you want to get high right now, but, long term, do you want to get sober?"

"I do."

"So, let's pretend, uh, by some magic circumstance, a dimebag falls from the sky and lands right in your lap—"

—Oh, sweet idiot, if only he knew—

"—Would you do it?"

I answer immediately, "No."

"Do you mean that, or are you just saying that because it's the right answer?"

"No. I mean it. I mean. I think I mean it. I don't know. I—don't know— I've been a fuck-up all my adult life—and I've been on drugs all my adult life. And all my adult life has felt pointless and trivial and hopeless. I do coke because it makes the world make sense. So—maybe it's a tough place to get to—and a lot to ask of myself—but I'd like to wake up one morning to a life that makes sense. And if that's a life without coke, okay. *I'm here to try it.*"

I've got this weird pinch in my neck; I don't know if it's a mosquito or if it's the painful fact that I might have just meant what I said.

A whimpering erupts from the spot beside me. It's Oscar, he's already crying. It's every night with this fucking guy.

"Oscar," Cheesewheel points to him. "Want to share with the group what's on your mind?"

He can't even string a sentence together, he's already drooling. He has to pause and suck wind just to manage a single word, *"Today, when— we were—at—the bottom of The Eustace Green —It was—after lunch—I looked up—and I saw him—I saw God—Up at the top of the mountain—At first I thought—maybe it was another hiker—like a guy with—long hair and a beard—but no it was him—it was Jesus Christ of Nazareth—he appeared to me—in a vision."*

Anesh rubs circles in Oscar's back like he does every night.

"Well, that's sure inspiring," Cheesewheel chimes. "Although, if you're seeing visions it might be a sign of exhaustion—"

"No! This wasn't a hallucination it was—divine intervention—"

He collapses into his hands and it sounds like, I don't even know what he sounds like, like a Chipmunks album played backwards on low speed. I can't stand it. Fuck it, I think, I'm gonna do my coke.

"Hey, McAdams, I'm gonna go for a piss."

"Okay, but don't be long—and don't—don't wander too far from the firelight. There's poison ivy out here, it's everywhere."

I sulk away, into a maze of branches and thorns. The voices fade.

Anesh first: *Wait, on Eustace trail, yeah I saw that guy too, but that was just some guy with a beard. He had on Wayfarers and, like, a dog? I'm sorry bro, but I don't think that was Jesus.*

Then Cheesewheel: *Let's not take away Oscar's vision. Oscar, what did it mean to you when you saw Jesus on the mountain?*

I walk until the firelight is a red star beyond the trees and I can't hear any more of their moronic blubbering. I put the coke baggie in my hand and I shine my dollar store flashlight upon it. It sparkles. It twinkles. Like gold, like the cosmos, like—like a bag of powdered feel good should sparkle.

This bag is empty, really. It's emptier than an empty bag. It's a blackhole wrapped in plastic. Escape. *Sense. Light.*

I think about the drip; the acid hole at the back of the sinus, where bliss trickles in with the flavor of burnt bleach and diesel.

I rub the plastic. I feel like there's a tractor beam guiding the residue for my gums, but I fight it. I could snort this whole bag in one go. I really could. I might die. Maybe that wouldn't even be so bad. At least I'd be off the Appalachian trail. The fiend is doing somersaults in my guts. He's furiously clawing at my liver the way a cat tears away at an old couch. *DO IT* he shrieks. Rail it. Shred it. Swallow the bag. Get yegged and let the consequences be damned.

I open the bag and smell. Highway stink. My finger rubs the rim. Just one bite, I think. Just one pinky in for the booger sugar—but—

It pains me to do this. It physically pains me to act like the bubbly-bath, squeaky-clean, good-boy, boy scout— but I turn the bag sideways.

The coke tumbles out in chunks and wafts of cloudy dust. Like snowfall, some of it is taken on a light breeze, the rest spreads into the fresh mud before my boots. White turns to gray turns to brown.

The fiend crawls up from my guts, he uses my ribcage as a ladder and squeezes up my throat. He swims through my brain until he's right up in my ear.

He whispers, *"You could always come back later. It's just a little dirt. You can still snort it. Walk away, sure, but you can come back. Tonight, while the fools sleep, we can come back and we can snort it straight from the dirt."*

I spite him. My fiend. I take my boot and I smoosh the coke, deeper and wetter until it's an un-snortable coke mud.

—

I come back from the darkness. The fire is warm and I feel like a dope. Oscar is done crying and I've come in at the tail end of Anesh's turn.

"—But, like, maybe that's why we put the work in," he mutters. "Like—we—struggle because we know what's right. It's like you talked about, Mr. McAdams. Inside of us there are two wolves and—*it'slikeum*, we just gotta feed the good wolf until, like, the good wolf is like, powerful enough—and like—amped up—so that he can, like, kill the evil wolf—like with his claws and shit."

"That's very good Anesh," Cheesewheel folds his hands together. "Very graphic, but good,—Alright, before we call it a night, I thought it would be nice to go over the game plan for tomorrow. You might have heard me mention that we are a tad off course, so, I know you don't want to hear this, but tomorrow we're gonna have to make up for some lost time —"

I stop listening to Cheesewheel when I notice Desmond stabbing me with his eyes. They reflect back the fire. He's trying to assess if I sampled his USA coke. He stares so intensely I can hear the question.

No, I tell him, just by shaking my head. *No*. I poured the coke out. Every gram. Every spec. I'm going clean. My apologies to the cigarette manufacturers of America.

Cheesewheel drones on, "By Wednesday, mid-morning, this should take us up to Minton's Pass. A particularly lovely trail, some call it the Old Mint River Trail, and for you history buffs, it actually has some stops we can take relevant to Civil War weapons smugglers, *oooh*, exciting, I know —now— "

A twig breaks.

This is something you never want to hear in the middle of nowhere. It happens beyond our camp, the sound not originating from any of us in the party. It stops Counselor McAdams in the middle of his paragraph. Every head crooks to the same black patch of woods from where it originated.

The Counselor chuckles. "Must be an owl or something—*spooky*— Tomorrow night we'll probably end up camping just South of—"

He turns his head back towards the fire and—that's when it happens. A figure barrels out from the woods. It's not human. My first instinct is that it's an avalanche. It's mount Eustace collapsing in an earthquake. Formless black: it erupts from the trees and consumes Counselor Cheesewheel like a tidal wave. He squeals as it tackles him to the ground near the campfire.

Reality seems to— disassemble. There are too many moving parts to assess it all at once. Desmond falls backwards and collapses into the top of a tent. Oscar goes in to help the counselor, but scatters the campfire as he does so. Anesh simply rolls into the fetal position— and me, what do I do? I don't know what I do. I sit, perfectly frozen, my heart buzzing in my neck and my legs nailed to the ground.

I watch as this figure, this boulder, this stray storm cloud of perfect dark, eats my rehab camp counselor. In the now flickering light of a scattered fire, this monster reduces the Cheesewheel to shredded reams of cheddar. A hand is chomped clean off, right at the wrist. A wad of hair and section of scalp are pulled off as neatly as the skin from a fried chicken drumstick. As the counselor fights to escape, his clothes are ripped. In a matter of seconds he is without a shirt or jacket, and instead of clothes, the avalanche rock is ripping off sheets of skin, about the size of a standard US letter, and sliding them down a wet gullet.

A bear? No? Too sleek. Too thin. It's a cat? A panther? A bobcat? No. It's too god damn big!

It doesn't make sense to me. It's a…I see stripes. Bloody whiskers. A tail like a swinging firehose. Stripes of gold and black and white belly.

It's a fucking tiger. Like— the thing from the cereal box. A tiger. A tiger out in the middle of Appalachia; a nightmare hybrid of an alleycat and a great white shark. And big. I could have never guessed how big a tiger could get, but, god damn, this thing's the size of a Winnebago.

I'm still frozen; I watch in disbelief as Oscar tries to fist fight this damn thing like he's Siegfried and/or Roy. The tiger munches away at the counselor while Oscar, who, mind you, is a retired construction worker and has the biceps to prove it, just wails at the tiger's skull. The jungle cat is never even phased. Eventually, Oscar tries going for the tiger's eyes; this is when the tiger has had enough.

Muscles move under the tiger's fur like metal gears, and with a mouth still full of McAdams skin, it stands up on its hind legs, yeowls, and bitch slaps Oscar. Oscar's head spins clean backwards with a roman numeral three struck into his cheek. Several teeth fall out of his open maw before his body hits the ground with a hard, dead thud.

It's enough to get my legs moving. *"Oh, Fuck!"*

I try to stand but my legs are freshly boiled spaghetti noodles. All I can do is crawl backwards from the scene and stare helplessly as the tiger tosses around McAdam's limp corpse like it were nothing more than one of those inflatable dancing guys outside car dealerships.

A hand touches my shoulder, it's Desmond, he has only just freed himself from the nylon tent.

"We gotta run," he tells me. "Get up, Get up!"

He pulls me onto my feet. I turn towards the woods, but then turn back. I see Anesh. Curled up in the fetal position by the dying fire. Desmond tries to pull me into the woods, but, I stay planted.

"Anesh, we can't leave Anesh!"

It occurs to me that this may be the first time in my life I've ever been brave or selfless. I move into this warzone and slug myself to Anesh. He has his face buried in his knobby knees. He trembles.

I shake him. "Anesh, Anesh! We gotta run!"

Suddenly there's heat. And it's not the fire; it's the wet heat of a mouth. It's the tiger. He's coming in for a big, wet kiss. I turn my head to face yellow teeth; the size of fucking Doritos. They are caked with brown cavities and fresh blood. Little chunks of Counselor Cheesewheel hang between them like white corn niblets. A pink nose drips, a hammy tongue stretches out.

I guard my own face as I fall backwards. The tiger wasn't coming for me though, he was coming for Anesh. He tears into his torso like a stoned college kid into a pan of cinnamon buns. It's astonishing how fast it happens, how easy it is for the Tiger. The claws, the mouth, they dig so effortlessly past Anesh's t-shirt and into belly-flesh.

All the while, Anesh holds the fetal position, like they probably taught him to do in the event of a bear attack. Elbows at his ears. Eyes shut tight. Hands over his head. Anesthetized by adrenaline; he doesn't even know he's being gutted.

Claws rip the skin so effortlessly as Anesh is disemboweled through a hole at his side and beneath his rib cage. Gooey organs in colors of fuchsia and purple and blue pour out like easter eggs on a nest of glistening intestines and sputtering, ambiguous inside fluids that remind me of beef stock. The tiger paws through it as if looking for the extra tasty bits.

It snarls and it snarfs. A sound like a giant pulling snot from its nostrils. A deafening, firecracker purr.

Desmond grabs me again, pulling me by my biceps into the woods. *"Run or die you fucking idiot!"*

———

Movies make it seem so easy to run in the woods, but the actual woods are not so pleasant to run in. Especially at night, and especially with a weak-ass flashlight. Every three feet is a wall of trees, or a sudden drop in elevation. Desmond and I don't so much flee the camp as we have a losing boxing match against thorns and branches and roots and bushes and spiderwebs.

We get fucked up by the woods. We get scratches and we tear up our rain ponchos. At least once I grab what is most definitely poison ivy.

But we don't stop. After seeing three grown men reduced to bargain bin chew toys, it's hard to stop.

It feels like we run for forty straight minutes, but, let's be honest here, my internal clock is not exactly functioning at its highest efficiency. We come to a freshwater stream. Cold, mountain water. We splash through to the other side where Desmond tumbles into the rocky shoreline and I tumble down beside him.

Save for the churning water, it's quiet. At least, I think it's quiet; I can hardly hear a thing over my own interstate-highway blood rush.

I shine the light all around, ever vigilant for a furry tyrannosaurus rex.

Desmond knocks my light down. "Quit that dude, you're gonna bring him straight to us."

I lower the light. Shapes move in the dark and the smudges play tricks on me. I try to settle my heart, but it's still pounding.

I finally ask the obvious. "What the fuck is a tiger doing out here?"

"Shit, that was Bumpy," Desmond says, and I can't help but think that's an odd thing to say.

We catch our breath, I count my lucky stars in the sky.

"*That was Bumpy*," Desmond says again.

It's such an odd word, it pisses me off and I just can't let it go. "Bumpy, what do you mean? The trail, the road—is that like slang for shitshow? What's Bumpy?"

"No—" he gasps for air—"*That was Bumpy the Tiger. That's his name.*"

"Bumpy the Tiger?" I blink and then blink again. "Oh, okay, I'm sorry. You know the name of the tiger that attacked us? What you two are —familiar? You're acquainted?"

"Yeah," he says, to my surprise. "Bumpy—he was kind of a—he's kind of like a pet once upon a time."

"I'm sorry?"

"The growers, the farmers—they live out here full time on the coca farms. Some overseas investors, they gifted us a tiger, you know, for security— for prestige."

"Like Scarface."

"Yeah, just like Scarface. And it was just an innocent thing at first. He was just like a dog, a dog that kept getting bigger and bigger. Then, somewhere along the way—the—the guys started giving him coke. A bump here and there—for shits and giggles. He was crazy for the stuff, it was—it was like catnip. They started calling him *Bumpy*. Bumpy the Tiger. Then a few years back he broke out of his cage."

My jaw falls open. I start asking several questions, but never get past the first syllable.

All I can manage is a recap of the facts. "Bumpy the Tiger, is a, what, a coke farm security tiger that your Appalachian Mountain cartel has gotten addicted to cocaine? And, what, he—he— stalks the Old Mint River for an easy fix?"

Desmond's eyes are wild. "Did you open the dimebag? You know, tigers, they got noses like sharks. He probably sniffed out the sample I gave you. It led him straight to us."

"Why, in God's name, Desmond, would you not warn someone about a cocaine addicted tiger before giving them a bag of fucking cocaine?"

"Lower your voice! I thought it'd be safe, because, man, Bumpy's supposed to be dead!" Desmond pauses and swallows air. "They told me Bumpy was dead. They told me they shot him last spring. He was coming around the trails, he was eating up the crops and chasing some of our smugglers. So, they put a bullet in him—at least that's what they told me—Fuck!"

I'm still not sure what to do with this information. I guess, at the end of the day, the revelation that this tiger is not some anonymous monster, but rather one with an interesting biography, really doesn't change the immediate gameplan.

"Alright—fuck this— we need to get out of here," I stand, Desmond does not. "We need to get out of the fucking woods. Do you have a phone? A map? Anything?"

"I left everything, all I've got is the clothes on my back. Why, you?"

"Just the flashlight—alright let's be smart. McAdams said that we were near a basecamp with a store. A campsite with people and food. That was—north—he was taking us, which way did we run?"

"Fuck if I know, man."

"Well, think about it, we were—" I try moving my hands around like those of a compass, but, it occurs to me that I don't know the first thing about cardinal directions. "If the sun set in the—east—where is the sun going to rise? Because that's west, right?"

"The sun sets in the west."

"Okay. Alright. Yeah. Okay—do you remember which way the sun set?" I would have no clue what to do with this information, even if he did remember. "Alright never mind— your people, the Old Mint River. You said they have a farm. A trail. Well, where's that?"

It's dark, but, I vaguely see it as Desmond rubs his hand on his temple. "Man, I told you: I don't know. I'd need a map. And I left the map behind."

I take command. "We'll just keep moving then. We'll keep going this way; eventually the sun will rise and we'll come across—something—campers or a highway or a cave or a building or a goddamn—something! —We can't just lie here and wait for that thing to come back."

"Calm down," Desmond says. "I'm getting up."

—

We continue on past the stream. There's a clearing and a trail beyond that. It's not labeled or anything, but a trail is better than fighting branches.

We follow what little light the moon gives us, conserving our flashlight battery. The woods are dull and the path is winding.

My head hurts. My rashes hurt. My stomach hurts. I get that funny kind of headache when your brain needs sleep but knows it won't get any —and of course there's this tension, I carry it in my neck, that any second that ten ton mammal-dragon could come galloping up behind me and pop my head like a watermelon.

"So—" I say.

"So?" Desmond ducks under a branch that's grown over the trail.

"Yeah, so—So, what's your story, Desmond?"

"How do you mean?"

"Well, two and a half weeks in and you never so much as told a lie. So, who are you—really?"

Desmond takes a pause before he responds. "I'm nobody."

"Alright. Fine. Then where are you from?"

He turns back to me for this answer, one I could have guessed. "*Nowhere.*"

"What are you, a pod person? The cartel grow you out of the soil?"

"As far as you're concerned," he says. "Sure, why not?"

"You won't tell me anything?"

"It's best we save our breath."

—

We walk all through the night. There's this odd moment where time slips away from me. I'm slogging down this narrow trail of ankle-deep mud, and it's dark, it's the darkest it's been all trip. Then, my head bobbles and three hours are just *gone*. Suddenly I'm on a wide, rocky trail. A grayish sunrise is creeping in through the forest floor. I don't know if it's sleep or brain damage, but I'm happy to be out of the night.

I point in the direction of the sunrise. "So that's west."

"East. *The sun rises in the east.* Remember what I said?"

"Okay—well—does that help us any? Do you know where we are?"

We stop, and holy shit, every muscle in my legs shriek when we do.

Desmond scans the brush. It's the same brush from Georgia. It's all been the same. Tree trunks and shadows and the choir song of cicadas. Desmond lifts a finger and he quietly points down trail from us; to the right and beyond a steep curve, there is a mountain wall with two jagged tops.

"I think so," He says.

"You think so?"

"Yeah, I think so."

Without further explanation, Desmond resumes walking and without a better choice, I follow.

—

"I see something."

The words hit me like an alarm clock. I'd been sleepwalking again. The world comes back to me. I'm on another trail, one of intensely green grass and black-trunk trees that have moss growing on them like sores and scabs.

Desmond forces me to stop, he puts a hand out. "There, do you see it?"

My vision is blurry. I see: green and gray. Everything is camouflage.

Desmond keeps pointing, he whispers. "Just beyond the tree line, off the trail, there's orange—it's a tent!"

He jolts, erupting into an all-out sprint; I struggle to keep up.

Whatever Desmond saw finally comes into focus after a hundred meter dash. Just off the trail is a nylon tent, a nice one, sewn with materials of flashy blue, orange and silver.

The closer we get, the messier it all seems. There's trash scattered around the campsite— as I roll around the clearing, I see an abandoned backpack. It leads my vision to the tip of a pony-tail and then a pale hand.

"Hello!" I scream for all of heaven and earth to hear.

Desmond shushes me, holding a hand at my face. "—Look!"

Turning the clearing, I see the rest of it. This isn't a campsite, not anymore; it's leftovers from someone's midnight snack.

Bumpy was here. It might as well be written in blood on the side of the ripped open tent.

Two campers are sprawled out. Butchered. The bodies here are of a woman and a man. A veritable Garden of Eden; the two rest neatly beside one another, mirrored in the same face-up, hands out position. They wear high-end camping clothes. The woman wears only one of her expensive mountain boots; the man is halfway out of his puffy jacket vest. These details are trivial; however, as the much greater spectacle is these people's faces—or the lack thereof.

Both of these former human beings have been left without an identity. Their heads have been caved in, like kicked in pumpkins. There is yet a hairline and the point of a chin, but everything between is one bright-red mouth, a maze of gore and teeth and bone. On the man I spy a single eyeball, it hangs beside the ear. On the woman I spy a pierced nose resting curiously undisturbed a few feet from her gashed up hand.

"Fuck." It's the only thing I can say.

Desmond shushes me again.

While I stand, frozen in total shock at the sign of these obliterated corpses, Desmond gets straight to work. He hops into the tent and produces a canteen of water and some wrapped granola bars. He puts these things into my hands.

"Eat, drink," he whispers softly, quieter than the cicadas. "*Be merry.*"

He chugs water from another canteen as he rummages through the decedents' last effects.

"What a way to go," I say at a new, low volume, only to myself.

Desmond picks through bags and then rifles through piles of dead leaves. "You see a cell phone? A walkie-talkie, anything like that?"

I haven't seen anything. I haven't really been looking. I can't stop staring at the faceless Adam and Eve. On the woman, beyond the place where eyes should be, is an area of cracked skull. A corner of brain pokes out. It's not pink like you would expect; more orange and white. I've never seen a brain before: the human computer, the mind meat. It's humbling, really. It makes me feel small. It makes me want to throw up. It's a physically disgusting existential crisis.

"Rich Kid," Desmond snips. "Do you see anything useful?"

"No—" I say, the answer leaving me like a soft, involuntary belch.

I blink. "There's some stuff in the backpack, over there."

Desmond rushes over to the camping bag beside the woman. Closer than I would care to get to her. He flips the backpack over to find it's been eviscerated too, ripped neatly down the middle. Pouring out from this tear is not clothing or camping supplies, but bricks wrapped in yellow plastic. One of the bricks has been torn open, it spills white powder.

Desmond licks his pinky and dips it in, then he rubs his gums and swishes it around.

"Yeah, that's our stuff."

Now, I'm not here to brag, I knew some properly terrifying dealers back in my day—but—let's be real here; the most coke I ever saw at one time could still fit in a fast food cup. This dead smuggler's backpack is filled to its breaking point with bricks, plural, of uncut, bleach-white cocaine. Pounds of the shit. *Gallons.*

The world falls away. Desmond, the corpses, the woods. Even the sky and the earth. It all fades to black. I'm left in a void with this glowing backpack of snow. I bite my lower lip so hard that it almost bleeds. A light gust of wind comes and sparkles just the tiniest taste into my nostrils. I drool.

I am struck with memories of childhood, when a gameshow would advertise that tantalizing *life-time supply* of some candy or soda, and, what a religiously awesome concept that was; here I am, a grown man, with that same awestruck wonder of a *life-time supply*. There's enough coke in this backpack for me to drown in it. To carry me to eternity. I shudder. I go weak in the knees.

Desmond feels around the belt-line of the female corpse. Before I can ask him what he's doing, he unsheathes a hunting knife from her belt. He digs the knife into the coke brick like a cereal spoon and brings it straight to his nose. He snorts. A deep, satisfying vacuum suck. In an instant, his pupils expand to the size of quarters.

He huffs and offers the knife up to me. "It's not safe to travel with any of this stuff on us. If you want a taste you'd better do it now."

"I—" I have to close my eyes. "I shouldn't."

"You're probably still in withdrawal. Medically speaking, your best chance for survival is to take a little bump."

What I don't say to Desmond is that it simply wouldn't be possible to take a *little* bump. Not with a millennium's worth of coke lying right there for the taking. No, I know the devil inside me. I know the creature that lives within the prison of my flesh. One bump and I'd be trapped here. One little bump and I would just curl up inside that backpack like a babe returning to the womb, and I would just snort and snort until my blood was the color of strawberry ice cream.

I refuse. Drooling, white-eyed, sniffing out of psychosomatic nostalgia; I refuse with a tiny nod side to side. Desmond carefully washes the knife with canteen water and places it into his own pocket.

"Alright, let's check these bodies for a phone and then let's get the fuck out of here. Why don't you search Antonio for me?"

"Antonio?" I ask.

Desmond is already on top of the faceless woman, like he's riding cowgirl. He's rummaging through the dead woman's pockets.

"That's Antonio. *Him.* I've met these two before I think." Desmond explains. "Antonio and Katie. They run the product to the trucks."

"Oh."

"They were a couple. Just got married too."

"*Oh*, oh that's sad."

"Sure—Now, check Antonio for a phone."

It takes some willpower, but I put my body to work and crawl over the body of the man with a collapsed head. Somehow, him having a name makes it all worse. I try not to look at—*Antonio*— as I work through his still-warm pockets, but, of course, I take a peak. How can I not? This close up, there're so many more horrid details. A tongue is glistening with spit. A blood-painted ear hosts a gold cross. He still has his bottom teeth, the top are in a mangled nest of head innards that look like a smashed pomegranate, Nearby the remnants of an eyebrow are still frozen in terror on a patch of skin the size of a debit card.

I check the pocket of his vest and—something squishes out Antonio's face. It's like a fountain spurt of black and yellow bile. It comes out of what was once a mouth. There, beyond former gums and former lips is a toothy meat cave, where the throat begins—it squirts and felches.

Is it gas escaping the corpse?

"Desmond?" I say.

Antonio's head moves. A left arm adjusts. Antonio isn't a corpse at all.

"Desmond!"

He's panicked. "What? Is it Bumpy?"

I take a few steps back. "No, it's your friend. I think he's alive. Oh! Shit! Yep. Oh, he's alive. Oh fuck!"

Desmond takes the place beside me, and it's obvious he wants me to be mistaken, but Antonio just keeps squirming. Who knows how aware this guy is, peeled down to two of his five senses and in shock, but there he is: alive, mind in total darkness. He writhes. His shoes scrape in the dirt. He bleeds. He hurts. He suffers a suffering I couldn't even begin to comprehend.

Antonio tries to speak. This sounds about as pleasant as you can imagine. What's left of a jaw and a tongue meekly whip about as a black hole pussy makes red and yellow bubbles.

"We need to get him to a doctor." I say. "We-we-we-we-we need an airlift."

"No," Desmond says.

He wraps his fingers tight around his new knife. "We need to put him out of his misery."

"You can't be serious."

"Well, did you find a phone? Can you get us an airlift?" Desmond looks at me with a distinctly yegged intensity.

I recognize that manic confidence; he's already made up his mind.

"Imagine that was you," Desmond asks, "Would you want to keep on living like that?"

"Yes! Yes I would. I would always like to be alive if the alternative is death—"

"After your face has been eaten off? You'd want to keep on living?"

"Sure! Helen Keller did fine. There's plastic surgery and, I don't know, they've got computers that let you see and stuff! And— I don't know!? Face transplants? I mean, you watch enough daytime TV you see plenty of people get their faces eaten off and they go on to—to be *inspirational speakers*—and write books! And—and live full lives! And— This dude is your coworker. I mean, you know this guy. How can you— how can you—we need to get him to a doctor!"

"We don't have a doctor. He's blind. He's dumb. He's probably deaf. For all we know he's concussed. If you want to get him medical attention, we're gonna have to carry him, and we don't know where the fuck we are. We'd be walking around at half a mile an hour with a guy with tiger-bait for a face. I don't know where you got your fucked up idea of becoming an inspirational speaker, but if that were me lying there, mutilated beside the love of my life, I'd beg whoever found me to cut my throat."

My own throat clicks. "So, what, are you gonna do it?"

He licks his upper lip. "Well, you're not gonna do it."

"No—"

A twig snaps. Somewhere else. This is not an extraordinary noise, but, when you're as paranoid as I am right now, you hear a sound like that and you spin your head whatever direction it needs to go.

I spin my head back to the green trail, and there is what I at first think is a vehicle. A great, striped bus barreling at 90 miles an hour. My eyes adjust and, of course, this is Bumpy; bulky gorilla tabby cat. He moves with a near impossible speed, sleek with ears retreated and claws out. Agile and delicate movements, almost unreal, like one of those Chinatown dragons with a dozen agile dancers under it.

Now, by daylight, I can see his battle damage. This is an old, battle ravaged tiger. Bumpy's been shot a few times in the head. There're perfect circle holes in his ears and wounds around his snout. They form old green scabs, like those on the trees; no fur grows there. One eye is dilated to a black pearl with the thrill of the hunt. The other eye is faded to a pale blue marble.

I fumble for escape right over the bodies of Antonio and Katie. Desmond fumbles with me as we retreat into the woods.

"Get down," he tells me.

"What?"

Desmond grabs me by the collar of my shirt and he yanks me down. We take cover behind a fallen oak tree not thirty feet from the crime scene.

"Don't—move—"

Desmond mouths these words to me. My heart palpitates; every beat is as loud as a fucking car accident.

I listen as this two-ton cocaine beast descends upon the campsite. I am relieved to hear the sound of sniffing, and claws pulling at junk. Bumpy didn't see us. Not yet anyways.

"*What's he doing?*" Desmond asks.

I poke one eye above the log. Bumpy has his teeth around Antonio's ears and neck. He shakes him about; lazily finishing him off.

"*He's putting your friend out of his misery.*"

When Bumpy is done playing with his leftovers, he rummages through the coke bag. It would make a cute internet video if it wasn't for all the blood and corpses; this big fuzzy goober poking around with bricks of snow. It seems Bumpy doesn't grasp the concept of snorting; instead, he rips into the bags with his claws and munches on piles of coke like it's sugar.

Desmond asks, "*What about now?*"

"*He's—getting his fix.*"

I swear—Bumpy almost hears me. His head rises with ears perked, gums are powdered white, nose is dripping a gray-color juice. The one good eye is wild; the pupil expands to encompass the entire eye.

When I check back, seconds later, he's resumed his buffet. He munches coke by the pint, only pausing to breathe.

"*Alright, look man. I think I know where we are now,*" Desmond begins—

"*You think?*"

"*Yeah, I think.*"

He bites his lower lip and stares upward, it's like he's trying to read the inside of his own brain. "*If that's Katie and Antonio, that means we're on the old Mint River Trail—and if that's Minton's peak up there, that probably means the site behind us was their stop on their first night. If I remember the map right, that just means it's about nine miles west of the coca farm compound.*"

"*The compound? Fuck your compound, Desmond, I want real people. Not a drug lord's summer camp—*"

"It's a forty mile hike back to civilization—And that civilization is nothing but a trailer park. You might not like it, but, right now, our best bet is to go west to the Old Mint River compound. The farm has guns. Cabins. Food. First aid kits. Beds—"

"Alright already, alright, shut up already, you've sold me. How do we get there?"

His eyes roll back once more; he's trying hard to remember. He unfurls his hand and tries to figure west from east.

He subtly points, a left turn from the trail we were just on. *"There ought to be a trail through that opening. It will go up Minton's peak. We'll go up, go around the mountain and come down the other side and then, after a few miles more, we'll find the compound."*

My sixth sense tells me to check on Bumpy again.

The big guy is still ears deep in the coke bag. Maybe he'll OD, I think. Farley himself. But no. He pulls out and chews with his maw towards the canopy. He's so pumped he's practically glowing radioactive orange. His paws tremble. His lips purse and kiss the open air as he sucks off the last residue from his lips and whiskers.

Suddenly, he does that thing cats do: I had an old girlfriend call it the zoomies. This cocaine tiger just starts tearing shit up. He pounces at invisible targets, he turns an oak tree into a scratching post. Then he roars, and it's a movie sound. It's an eardrum shattering bellow, the kind of sound a dinosaur makes. The trees and all the branches shutter at the king of the woods.

I remember that feeling. I've had more than a couple nights where I felt just like Bumpy.

The big guy lays down on his back, right between his last victims.

"I think he's blissed out—we should move—while he's distracted."

—

Desmond and I hike. It's not an easy trail, but the weather is forgiving. We hike straight upward, one unforgiving hill after another. Fields of dull gray rocks, like poorly sculpted cemeteries.

I don't try talking to him. It would be a waste of energy.

Eight miles doesn't sound like much. What is that? A thirty minute drive? A half of one single second at cruising altitude on a jumbo jet? But the miles move slower on blistered feet and a brain that hasn't slept.

We don't rest. It seems unwise to rest when Bumpy could wake up any moment and smell us down to the exact inch.

So we walk. Like we did every day before. And we never stop walking. We walk up hills, valleys, over streams and then the start of a mountain and around a mountain's face, through so much mud and so many wood stripe tunnels. The same dirt. The same insects. The same cramps and rashes and blisters and bruises.

—

The day runs away. It's almost evening now. The sun is in the earliest stages of shifting from white to dusk's orange. My brain feels like an egg that's somehow been pickled, fried and hard-boiled.

After a rise in incline, we come across a vista. It's magnificent really. Five boulders extend to make a diving board above the canopy. It's like a fucking greeting card; an ocean of neon acres, Appalachia goes on forever like some magic kingdom, on until the trees become a hazy green slime that fades into the farthest reaches of baby-blue daylight.

Endless nature. Not a human being or a building as far as the eye can see.

We do stop here. At long last. It's like some kind of caveman instinct. I climb to the end of the farthest reaching cliff and I sit. I let my beat-to-shit legs dangle in open air.

Desmond stands, only a few feet behind; he hands off the water canteen.

"Last sip," he says. "It's yours."

I don't hesitate to drink it down. "What, am I starting to grow on you?"

"No, you need it. You're older. You're less experienced."

"Older—*I'm in my thirties*—" I wipe my chin. "—So, how far away are we?"

"Home stretch," he says with a hint of faith.

"That could mean anything. A Mile. Five. What?"

"It means home stretch. I'm talking thirty minutes tops."

I take a hard breath, the air is thin. "So, it's almost over?"

"—Not out of the woods yet."

I don't know if that was a joke or not. I don't laugh either way.

—

It's easier to move now. Hope works like that or maybe it's the lack of oxygen. My head is empty, my lungs whine, every inhale snaps and crackles like fresh cereal in milk. We come to a fork and take the right-hand path. It takes us down the mountain. The bobbing of momentum gives me a headache, but I remind myself not to complain. Soon there will be a bed and a roof. If I'm lucky, a private toilet. I imagine a white hippie chick with hairy armpits. You know, the kind of girl who would live on a weed farm (maybe there's a coke variety of this kind of girl). Maybe she's got blue hair. Maybe she falls in love with me and nurses me back to health and she's got great tits and I sleep on them.

It's gonna be hard to stay sober on a cocaine farm, I think. But I push the thought away. I'll conquer that beast when I'm safe from the other one.

—

We slog. The headache gets unbearable, sharp and dull at the same time; the headache drips down until it's in my toes and fingertips.

"Talk to me," I say to Desmond.

"About what?"

"I don't know. Just—say something. I'm starting to feel like I might faint."

Desmond points at a spot in the skyline, a particularly tall tree upon a hill, two football fields away.

"See that tree? On the skyline. The compound is just on the other side of that."

It's getting hard to breathe, I have to pause between my words. I think it's the heat and the thin air. "Cool— Cool. Still. Tell me a story or something. Tell me—*Tell me something*."

"What?"

"I don't know, man. Recount your favorite episode of The Simpsons. Tell me a dirty joke. Fuck, just, recite the ABC's. Something."

He says nothing. He walks. I inch behind in his shadow, rapidly deteriorating at the finish-line. I need conversation to stay awake.

"What's your name?" I ask.

"You forgot?"

"No. I just figured your identity is fake. Your addiction is fake. Why wouldn't your name be fake too? You don't even look like a Desmond."

"—And what is a Desmond supposed to look like?"

"I dunno—not you."

He lets the conversation die again, but I can't let him off the hook. "Okay. So what is it? Mike? Malcolm? No, you don't strike me as an 'M' guy. Charlie? Are you a, uh, a Frankie?"

"You're just gonna guess?"

"You could always tell me."

He turns back, first time I've ever seen this mystery fucker genuinely smile, "I don't have a name."

And it's the funniest thing, the funniest thing since a tiger ate Cheesewheel McAdams, but I believe him.

I do my best to chuckle. "Fuck you."

Something in the woods snaps. I've come to learn what this means. Desmond, or, *the man with no name*, turns back. His expression of utter terror spells it out perfectly. Bumpy is behind us; I turn and I see it too.

There's no stealth about his assault. He doesn't need stealth. We're too weak to warrant stealth.

Bumpy is not quite running, but falling down the mountain, again, like an avalanche. An avalanche of black and orange stripes. It almost seems like he's grown, he's somehow the size of a wide-load eighteen wheeler with a front grille full of steak knives. Bits of coke puff from Bumpy's face like steam from a locomotive.

One white eye shines, the other, once green, is now blackened with a cocaine-blissed pupil.

Desmond erupts into a sprint. He's younger, faster, better trained. He pumps his arms and I struggle to keep up.

Stitches form in my stomach. The nerves die off in my toes. My heart gets wonky. I might just collapse into death before Bumpy even reaches me.

Desmond pumps harder, he pulls out ahead, he's going to disappear soon. I'll be alone. I'll be one hundred and sixty pounds of jungle-grade meow mix.

Difficult as it is to form strategy through the fatigue and fear, a thought occurs to me. I remember— I've been taught precisely what to do in this situation.

I heard it in business school, back before the coke made me flunk out. Wasn't even a few years ago. The university invited my dad to give a speech for orientation, and he spoke, literally, *directly* about what to do when you're running from a monster in the woods.

I'd heard the same advice from high-school principals, coaches, college admissions counselors. It's the very adage of the American way; capitalism at its heart: *if you find yourself running from a bear in the woods, it's not about running faster than the bear, it's about running faster than the guy next to you.*

Sure the idiom usually refers to a bear, but the advice works for a coked up tiger in a pinch.

Without so much as a dimebag of remorse or hesitation, I use the last of my life force to sprint. I destroy the cartilage in my knees, I blow out my lungs, I use gravity to my advantage and I fall forward on the path until I pull up to Desmond's side. I take this momentum and put it into my fist.

Desmond turns to look at me, he probably thinks I'm about to share some bright idea with him, but no, I spin my upper body into one wicked punch that lands squarely on his nose.

It catches him off guard. He hobbles to a stop and when he's stopped completely, I do my best to make sure he stays that way. I knee him in the balls. Hard. Like they taught me to do to a prospective molester when I was just a boy in karate.

It all happens too fast, Desmond can't quite understand it. All he really knows is that something hit his face, his eyes close, and in that darkness his testicles suddenly explode. All he manages is a '*What the fuck?*'

For good measure, I push him to the ground. Desmond folds into a pile of dreads and sweat and pink pants, totally blind and completely emasculated. Bumpy is right upon us now. I turn and I run. I leave behind my sacrifice.

I know I'm safe when I hear Desmond's scream. He screams like a child after the drop of a roller coaster; this high pitch vibrato song. It shakes side to side as his body is shaken side to side, then, suddenly, the sound is muffled.

I check over my shoulder once, briefly pausing to catch my breath. It's hard to see it all happen through the branches, but it looks like Bumpy is giving Desmond mouth-to-mouth resuscitation. When Bumpy comes up from his first breath, Desmond no longer has a face. Nothing. No nose or mouth or eyes. He's been made faceless, same as he was nameless. From the distance, it appears as nothing but a T-bone steak framed by stray dreadlocks. Desmond, or whatever his name might be, is still alive though —I can tell as he blindly stabs at fat and fur with his knife. It sinks into

Bumpy, again and again and again, around the cheeks and neck—but the blade never even so much as phases him.

I stop watching. I run and I run and I don't look back.

—

I follow the trail to the point Desmond had instructed. Finally, around a corner, I come face to face with a fence, the kind that typically surrounds impound lots, construction sites and prisons. It is eight feet tall and chain-link, chrome coils of razor wire across the top.

A white sign reads PRIVATE PROPERTY; TRESPASSERS WILL BE SHOT.

"HELLO?" I scream.

On the other side of the fence is a narrow perimeter of trees and brush, but beyond them I can make the shapes of wood huts and cottages; a little secret village. I'll be damned. There really is a secret coke farm out here.

I shake the fence and it loudly rattles. "HELLO!"

Nothing.

I follow along the perimeter, hoping to find a gate or an entrance, even just a spot on the fence without razor wire coils.

I don't make it very long before I hear it. Raw power. A thunderstorm on four clawed feet. Bumpy is already finished with Desmond. He isn't about to let me go quietly. He's prowling in the trees. Over twigs and snaking between the trunks. He's on my scent. He can smell what little cocaine there is left in my sweat. He wants me. He wants to take away my face.

My legs are so weak that I have to use my hands to pull myself along the chain-links.

It might give my position away, but I scream anyway. I wrap my hands into the wire and violently shake, *"HELLO! PLEASE! SOMEONE!"*

I can smell Bumpy, pennies and spoiled hot dogs on his tongue. Cocaine on his breath. That kitty litter ammonia stink. A glance backwards finds him fighting through the last line of the branches.

It's at this point I have to stop and choose my fate. I can try to climb a tree, which will only prolong the inevitable, or I can collapse into the fetal position and have my spinal cord ripped out through my asshole. Or I can run, but, I don't have another teammate to sacrifice.

There is a fourth option, I realize. I glance upward, where the wire fence tops out at a bushel of impenetrable steel razor wire—how impenetrable is it, though?

I'm not sure which of these options is the best. Maybe I'm just fucked and all that's really left of my own free will is a decision for how I get fucked, but, eager not to end up like Antonio or Desmond or Counselor Cheesewheel, I jump onto the fence and climb upward, bravely into the reams of razor wire.

I hear Bumpy at the fence below me. I think he even sniffs my foot. He doesn't roar, but he exhales, somehow exasperated. Even Bumpy is baffled with the choice I've made.

He jumps. I don't see it, but I feel it. I feel the iron wiring move as the tiger stacks his massive weight into the chainlink.

I pull harder, upward, brazenly tugging my own body into the death hula-hoops. The gap between two rings is wide enough that I can easily fit my head, but, then, to go further, I have to squeeze my shoulders. On nothing but raw adrenaline, I force my upper body into the coils. It's like driving a loaf of bread into a slicer, only this loaf of bread is my mortal personhood. Three-inch-long and one-inch-deep knives cut into my shoulders, then my stomach, then my pants. They easily cut through clothing, and I'm surprised to find the blades oddly warm from a day basking in the sun.

It all just sort of—*happens*—This—*Hellraiser type shit.* The adrenaline guarantees I can't feel it. It's just like being at the dentist. Loops of razors fold, and pop back into shape, slicing at my cheeks, running blades down my wrist. I almost fall and must instantly grab a loop for stability; I grab directly on a blade and it neatly slices my fingers and palm.

I don't let this stop me. I ignore the pain and pull until my body is safely contained, horizontally laid into this fence top death-tube. I look down my body. My clothes are shredded and in some, maybe most, of those shreds are deep, deep, gashes. Long bleeding lines, like mouths, like the faces of ham sandwiches, and they gush this blood that's hot, and thin, and it's incredible how much of this blood there is.

I feel air against my cheek. Wet, hot.

Once again, I've find myself face to face with Bumpy. He's partially climbed the fence. His nose is at my nose. I can see the freckles in his one good eye. I can make the shimmering buckshot in his forehead. All that separates us is a loop of razor wire. He opens his death trap jaw. It stinks of hot roadkill. He tries to give me his patented French death kiss, but a razor wire loop gets in his way. It folds into his jowls and a section of blade cuts his tongue. The tiger pulls off from the fence with a frustrated snarl.

—

I'm sure the Cheesewheel would have had a metaphor for this. I'm sure he'd say Bumpy represents my yearning for coke, and the fence is— the fence is— sobriety, and the coils of razor-wire, why, those are the judgements of other people, or, maybe they are my own self-doubt. Or they're my tortured past.

Fuck the metaphor though; I feel wet and sticky. I look down and I'm completely soaked in blood and the stuff's starting to harden like super glue. It comes from a whole party of lacerations and drips into the dirt below like rainfall described in the Book of Revelation.

Blood pumps, steady, but not fast, out of my arms and my shoulders and my hands. I can't say how much, but it's more blood than I'd even guess I had. I mean, logically, if I saw that much blood I would assume whoever lost it was long dead, but here I am, thinking thoughts and being alive and bleeding, bleeding, bleeding.

My body is tangled like headphones in a junk drawer. I can't hardly feel it, there's too much to feel. My back is arched awkwardly over the fence-top, there's razor wire wrapped around my legs. One loop is collapsed below my back and its tension drives another loop into my crotch, into my belly, they cut deeper with every micrometer I move. The more I fight it, the more it holds me and cuts me.

Bumpy doesn't know quite what to do. He sits eagerly at the bottom of the fence near the blood pools where he wildly pants and drools and rocks back and forth like an excited kid waiting up for Santa to come down the chimney. He's waiting on a wrong move. He's waiting on me to fall.

I guess I should feel victorious. I guess I got what I wanted. I've survived death by coke tiger, but, at what tremendous cost? Here I will die. Seventeen days sober, fatality by razor wire fence.

I try to sit up, to straddle the fence top, but, the loop at my groin pops outward, it splits my shirt right down at the middle and takes a ribbon of flesh.

"FUCK! SOMEBODY HELP!"

I almost fall again, and for the second time, I grab hold of a blade. It catches my fingers, putting a neat slice across every single one of them.

—

The sky turns pink. The clouds turn gray. The woods, black.

It's beyond me how or why I don't pass out. But, as I continue to fight the bushel of razor wire it becomes clear to me that I should have let the tiger eat me. At least it might have been quick.

I manage to get on the opposite side of the fence, my body halfway out the death tube, but it's just about diced my legs, there's this one cut, the death cut, down the chest, it looks like the first cut of a frog about to be dissected. I swear I can see ribs.

I've had to pull out of my pants and jacket. They hang on the blades around me; shredded. I've lost my underwear and one shoe. I've only got on a t-shirt and it's totally soaked from cuts along my abdomen.

Bumpy yet waits. He watches me like I'm roast pig on a spit at a luau. That smell must be driving him crazy. You have to wonder if he prefers blood to coke.

I'm his television now. The one working eye follows my every movement. He slobbers at the sight of so much delicious man.

It's funny. I used to have a girlfriend with cats. The face Bumpy is making now is the face her cats used to make when she got out the can opener.

I find myself chuckling. *Oh, fuck me, what a silly and ridiculous way to die.*

I keep fighting my way out of the razor wire loops. Gentle. Slow. Eventually I fuck up though, I uncurl my leg from a loop, and try to sit my weight down, but there's a blade at my seat. It pops directly into the space between my legs, running right through my underwear and carving a lengthy second anus into me. I involuntarily yip, I jump. I fall.

I tumble from the fence. My foot catches a loop of wire and it spins me. I plummet eight goddamned feet, which doesn't sound like a lot, but, for me it's so long it feels like an entire red eye flight in coach. I land on hard gravel and the impact breaks my left forearm— Just snaps it like a breadstick.

I cry. I can't be blamed. I've never been much of a crier, but, if ever there was a reason to do so, it's this.

Bumpy throws himself at me. I feel the wind shooting out from his mouth. But I've fallen on the other side from him, I realize. He bends the chain link and grabs it with his raptor claws.

He can't get me. Not with a fence between us. I'm not his kill anymore. I've been killed by the damn fence. A broken arm under me and an almost naked body torn to shreds with a thousand weeping gashes; no Bumpy, I am not yours.

I crawl backwards, into a thin perimeter of woods, dragging the exposed and lacerated flesh of my ass through rocky gravel, a newly dead arm flopping at the side like a long, dead animal tied to my shoulder.

Bumpy watches me for a moment, licks his lips, and then he too saunters off into the woods. Off to find more blood or coke or faces to eat off.

I hobble to a stand. I remove my shirt and do my best to tie it around my gushing right arm where the cuts are worst. The blood coagulates and dyes the shirt brown. I move. I walk the best I can; it leaves a wake of thin red lines and drops.

—

I am completely naked, save for an arm sleeve and a single boot. The setting sun feels strange and radioactive against my open wounds. It quickly dries the wet blood. Turning it sticky and fading it to the color of shit.

Patches of my body are dyed muddy black, others pale, others pink, swollen, others run with cherry-Kool Aid rivers.

I wiggle my sock around in my one good boot and it's floating in a stew of body fluids.

I'm woozy. The blood was already thin, now it's in short supply. There's a haze over my thoughts. It feels like when the room starts to spin after too many tequila shots. That border state to a blackout. Only this is a blackout I won't wake up from.

I emerge out of the woods and onto the grounds of the Old Mint River Compound.

The camp itself is not what I had expected. I had imagined something out of a spy movie. Rolling hills and armed guards in bulletproof vests. My dying hope was a doctor and an infirmary, but, for all of Desmond's promises, this place here is meek; it is like a four acre summer camp. There are a few cabins about the perimeter, they are sloppily constructed of brick and lumber. A helicopter landing pad rests decidedly empty by an outdoor cafeteria. Center to it all is the coca farm.

Grown in even rows, the plant appears like holly bushes or mistletoe in lines of clay pots; the leaves only a dustier shade of green. They wouldn't be out of place on the lawn of a country club. Branches rustle with twigs of red coca berries. They wave softly in the wind.

"HELLO!—ANYONE?"

I identify the shape of a person; lying there under the shade of a coca plant. It's a corpse in blue jeans, with an AK-47 laying expended beside it. I peek beyond the branches. He's faceless; like the others. A mask of teeth, eyeballs, hair and bone in all the wrong places.

Bumpy's already been here. He's already massacred the whole farm. There's a line of bodies, I follow their shapes as they mark a trail of expended magazines and blood splatter leading to a wide-open gate at the property's end.

A wide open gate.

I got dissected for nothing. If I'd just run a little longer—just a few hundred feet, I'd have spared myself from dancing in the razor-wire hula-hoops.

"Shit," I cry, and I drool, and I almost fall down onto my knees, but I don't.

I hobble, falling with every step, leaking, as I make my way to the largest building here. It's a metal hanger on the other side of the helipad.

I collapse through a metal gate into its dry heat. The floor here is dirt; its walls are rusty metal. It has no lights, only a fading brown amber that pours in from the windows above.

It stinks. It reeks of gasoline.

This is the factory.

At the far left is what looks like the waste from a landscaping company. Coca leaves are gathered in brown bags. Beside them is a shelf of red jerrycans, and beside that is a collection of blue drums where picked leaves are actively soaking.

Further to the back, in the shadows, beyond a faceless corpse in scrubs and rubber gloves, is a great steel trough with sparkling white contents; a goddam bubble bath of white powder.

I spill my blood as I walk to it.

Beside a shelf of empty plastic bags, this trough is filled to its brim with finished product. Cocaina. *Love of my life.* The only thing that ever really, truly, made me happy. My only candle in the valley of shadows. My light in the darkness.

I laugh. Tears and snot-fused blood drip off my nose, but, I laugh.

With barely operating fingers, I gently touch the side of this trough. It's the size of a—well, it's the size of a coffin. A box fit for me.

I do not hesitate. I ease my body into the trough with the intent to drown like a cockroach fallen into an open sack of sugar. I sink my naked and lacerated limbs below the surface, burying them the way a child buries themselves in sand at the beach.

Excess powder overflows from the sides, while fresh, stinging coke, coagulates in my thousand open wounds, including my new womanhood. It enters my blood at a thousand ports. I remove my t-shirt-made-tourniquet and bury my split arm into white sand. Coke holds the arteries, the bones, the soul. The dark magic works its way to my heart, and in mere seconds I feel it shine as bright as a dying star.

It hits my heart. There's more coke in me than blood now. You could plug my heart into the municipal co-op and I could power a city better than any nuclear power plant.

But, oh, the brain. It's not in the brain yet.

I roll over and put my nose in. I suck. I suck on a breath I hope to die in. Coke soaks into my pores, my cuts, it sticks to the sweat and bleaches me into a white-skinned vampire. My eyes explode into black. Sweet, stinking, fuel shoots directly into my mind and I am left with only a taste; of bleach; of gasoline; of infinity.

There isn't a drop of blood in my body that isn't vibrating to boiling point. Tanner Jaffee is dead. He is in the darkness beyond the candlelight with Desmond and Antonio and Anesh and Oswald and McAdams and Katie. I am the fiend now; faceless demon of antiquity, more persistent than Bumpy and centuries older. When this body dies, he will simply move onto another junkie. I am but his temporary vessel; a nose through which to suck this wicked mana. For however brief this moment might be: I am the spirit of cocaine. It laughs with my borrowed mouth; a maniacal, uncut joy. A joy without spirit. A joy without will. A joy without pleasure, but certainly power. The sound of laughter echoes off the harsh surface of the metal factory equipment and bounces back at me. This is the song of that joy. A hymn.

It is interrupted by a puff of hot breath.

I glance up and find that I am once again face to face with Bumpy the tiger. No longer a fence between us. He'd come right in through the wide-open gate. One eye stares directly into mine. He hesitates before he opens his mouth—he reaches in. He licks me like a loyal dog welcoming his master home.

I swear, on what's left of my life; he smiles —and I smile back.

AMERICAN TELEKINETIC

Anjle Baby

This hear is a sewiside note. No April Foolin'. Don't go in the bedroom now, ain't notting there U need Cin

A cuple things

U can find my wallit & other pertynant dokumints on the kitchin conter

As for funral rekwests, i have but 2

1stly: send me to heven looking pretty. I wuld like to be barried in my raddlesnake skin hat & raddlesnake skin belt & as U mite pressume, my raddlesnake skin boots. All this & the wite sears sucker suit w/ the topazz undershert & the ruby rock bolo tie

2ndly: I haven't a care for how U deside to go about my funral service. U can spread my burny ashes at the locel alleeway behind a kirspy kreem for all I culd care. Alls I do ask is for a song. Wen U lower me, or, toss me to sea or watever it is U do w/ this old erthly coyle, I want U to play: The Hiwayman song— by the Hiwaymen

That there old rime always got me better than most peeple ever culd & Im partial to Jonnyies part about sailing arond the unyverse in a star ship. I think thems real nice words fors a man to be layd to rest to

X

Baby U always said it felt like there was a part of me I never let U C. Likes as if my shadow showed the shape of a diffrent man than the man wat stood befor U i always told U U was crazy but, Anjle Baby, U wasn't crazy at all

C hear; Im gonna tell U about sumthing. Im gonna tell U about that shadow & I need U to no Im not tellin no tall tail neether. U're gonna think I drank myself loonier than a Sundy skunk, but, read wat I rite U hear & reelly chew on it. Dijest it. Dijest these words hear & I think U'll no in Ur hart that it's all tru. Evry dammt word. crazy as it mite seem.

C, Anjle Baby, I had me Sikik powers

Yes M'am & it's not like them mindreading sikik powers. I mean— I don't think I had those. Sumtimes, at the Cirkly K, or, the WallyWorld, somebody wuld give me a dirty look & I culd fantly hear them callin me all manners or cuss words inside my own mind, but, I beleve that there to be notting more than most ordunary intoowition

No, I had the other kind of sikik powers; I culd move objeks w/ my mind.

Laff all U want, but, shit, babe, U sat w/ me at those weels. U saw those perls trip like no perl ever shuld. U saw the way I culd put 500 dollar$ on black like I was just collectin a paycheck

Fact of the madder is, I had me this power alls my life. Even since I was a little ankle biter running round Bethlahem, Alabama

I didnt like to talk to U much about my childlyhood, but that's on a count I's was born into rite feerce poverdy. My 1st home was a tin gardin-shack with hardly a dirt floor. Those was the days before Ma' took to working in the pancake house, so's our folk wern't even pancake-house-poor yet

But me's & my brother Donnie didn't no we was poor. Not wen we was real littlelike. If U'd have asked us we'd'a told U we was the luckiest kids on erth. We was hungry sumtimes, sure, but, we ran wild & wen Ur wild and Ur free U don't care about those comforts monie brings

All me's & Donnie ever needed was eachother & someplace to make mischif. We'd go car climbin at the county salvage yard or go swimming in the creeks. Sumtimes we'd make frends w/ stray dogs or shoot our slingshots at stray cats. Hell, I 'member a week we didn't do nothing but thro rocks at passing cars on the innerstate

1 thing we loved to do was movies. I gess I always been sumthing of a movie dude. Donnie & me'd go C them down at this place called the

dollar world; But we didn't pay no dollar to get in, we snuck in thru a hole in the fondeation

We liked to do it wen we was to sunburnt for nothin else on acount they hads them anartic air contiyners (plus there was all that free popcorn if U didn't mind fishing it out the trash)

I want to say it was 1978: I was 9 years old, so Donnie must have been 13. 12 maybe. I don't member like I shood, but the 2 of us snuck into this movie here called The Mind Men & Baby, that wasn't no good movie, it was a fierce stinker in fact, but that there movie changed my life. Its all about these 2 kids w/ sikik supperpowers. U now they culd make stuff move or explode all just by thinking about it and the whole back halv of the movie all about the goverrment trying to capture them. Now, little 9 year old me had never seen nothin like that befor; it was a whole new consept, this Telekenezus & Mind over madder kinda bufoonry

Nows I took that there idea home w/ me to our 1 room tin shack house, & I tell U, baby, my bed there was hardly more than a pile of old rags in the corner where two walls met. Now, wile Ma & Donnie took to sleeping, I layd awake thinking about whatif I had them supperpowers like in that movie & I desided why not just try? So's, there in ner darkness, that little nine year old me identyfid a rusty nail on the dirt floor & I tried it to lift it using nothin but waves cuming out from my brane

Now, I bet U evry little boy the hole world over has tried that there manuver— Probablys even little girls have tried it to. I put out my hand & made a bunch of blood shoot into my face, I skwint my eyes real tite, & I comanded that nail there to float off the ground & baby, wuldn't U now it, I gots the dammed thing to flinch a little bit

Turns out I had me supperpowers.

X

I gess there was no rime or reason why I was embued w/ this hear power. We didn't grow up downriver from no nukleur power plant or nothin like that. Ain't never been no word from Ma if my long lost daddy was some kind of soopersoldjer

Sicic powers was just sumething I culd do. It was randum, like being double jonted or getting struck by litening or running into a movie star at a convenyence store. U mite say god rolled his kosmik dice on me

Alls I rilly now is that I didn't think much of it that 1st time. In truth, I was mostly disserppointed. The kids in that Mindmen movie I Cn were making amoosement park rides run backwerds & making peoples skulls explode; wen about all's I culd do was get a nail to do a little shimmy

I thote—maybe this power was like a muscle—& I culd better myself at it thru practise. So, sumtimes, wen me & Donnie'd get home from the Auto salvage or a day of swimming, he & ma'd go to sleep & I'd lie awake & I'd try to move things about our homeshack. EZ stuff: Buttons and wadded up paper. Later on, I graduwaited to forks & spoons

The way it worked was like—almost like I had this big indvisble tenacle sticking out of my 4head & if I thote realreal hard I culd make the tenacle strech out & wrap round shit. If U'll pardon the boyish langwage, I took to calling this tenacle my *mindsnake*

Corss, a name like that makes it sound a hell of a lot more danjerous than it reelly was. Even at my peek performunce, I only had about four feet of reech & I hardly had the strenth to break a glass bottle. Even at my most skilt I culdn't handle nutting complecated & I never in all my life did figure out how to make shit float on thin air. Doin so wuld hurt to damm much

C, evry time I used my mindsnake it'd give me this big, mean, rite ugly headake. No nosebleed, like U wat C in the movies, it was all in my eyesballs. Felt like putting to much air in a tire; like using my power was gonna make my damm eyes pop out my hed

I took to calling those kinda headaches: the *biteback.* Sumtimes the biteback'd nock me rite into a deep sleep like I'd done got hit by a stray speedball. Probably wern't good for me neether. Them bitebacks are probably why I growed up so small. Probably why my brane is always so dang fuzzy. Prolly why Im so old already when Im not suposted to be so old.

I probly don't hardly halv to xplain this to U, anjel baby. U been with me all these years. U Cnt me age 2ce as fast as a man shuld. U Cn me get sick after a nite of gambling. No, it wernt just the licker slowing this old boy down

X

U no, time passes like time dos & time changes shit. Like who U spend that time with.

Back in Bethlehem, used to Donnie wuld look out for me, but came a day, wen he found himself far more incherested in fe-male anatomee than playing big brother & alls a suddenlike I was left to run wild on my lonesum

& I mite have had me suppepowers, but, a lonesum boy I yet was. Schooling, of corss, made things no better neether

It mite shock U to learn I was not always the handsum devil U came to luv. In tru fact, I grew up stranj in my appearence. Small & ratty. Yes M'a'am. Kids at skool used to call me Eggboy cuz of my giant hed & the way I smelled like a rotten coup. That, & I used to wear this white shirt w/ red stripes, & our local chikken farm sold egg cartons w/ red & wite stripes. I don't now if that had anytheeng to do w/ it. Point is: I was no elementry skool presedent

To small for sports & to ugly for girls & to poor for fancy toys; I had me a lot of time alone in my pre teend years & wat did little eggboy do w/ his alone time? Well, he tried to refine his sikic powers on the debreese of the county's auto salavadge yard

I'd get out of skool feeling sour & sorry & I'd go to the salvadge and I'd ping lug nuts round with my mindsnake & sum times wen I'd get reel reel angry, I'd break reerview mirrors & windshielts. Sumtimes I'd use my power to hard & the biteback wuld nock me clean uncoshuss. I'd wake up in the middle of the nite restin in sum burnt out old Shevy. Have to walk home in the dead of the dark

Wern't good days. Wern't happy days. Wern't a happy kid

X

I never did tell nobody about my mindsnake. Not even Ma' or Donnie. I always thote if the secret got out, then maybe the govt wuld try to make me join the milatary & if I had to join the milatary they'd probably cut my hair. That or cut my branes open. Thats what movies have led me to beleeve. So, didn't nobody now about my mindsnake & by the time hiskool rolled round, this hear power went from secret to dubble secret on acount I begun using it for petty crimes

Now, picking pockets proved to complycated a task for my uncordynated mindsnake, but, making a girls skirt fly up, why, that I culd manaje just fine. I tell u baby, when that spring air first came arond, I probly did some serious brane damage doing the old Marylynn Munroe trick on damm near every skirt I saw (A dirty dog I was! U no my love of yung skin baby!)

Then, there was vending macheens, now, baby, thems were my first real conjob. We had this cola macheen in the cafayterya of our hiskool &s if I stood next to it & reelly focused I culd wind my snake up the drink-hole, & up into all them gears &—click. Drop me 5, hell, 10 free sodypops

Sumtimes I'd sell those suckers for cheaper than the vending macheen did; it was a cwick way to make me sum dimes & kworters; enuff for a burger on the walk home at least

Corss, the biteback always made it hard to focus on my afternoon studies & after using the snake to much I'd have to sleep thru a number of classes to reconsort my mentle enerjies. This hear mite offer sum explination for my pisspoor report cards and my lowsy spelling

X

After he got out of prison for assolt, Donnie got hisself a job towing trucks in Birminham & he'd send a share of his monies back to ma'. Ma' got herself a job to in this time (down at the pancake house) & pretty soon she was able to rent us a place w/ floors & a roof & a shower – & I had me my own bedroom like a normal kid. 15 years late but late's better than never

That old house was held together by nutting but chipped lead paint & spiderwebs, but it was a home goddammit & a dammed fine home at that

And after I got me my first real house, I got me my first real lover. That was in my Jr. Year. Sarah Mirth was her name. Or Maybe Sarah Myrtle. I met her selling stolen sodas & tho I was a petete boy, I wood her with my rugged outlaw charm. Ours was a brief effair consisting of no more than a few backseat heavy pettings in her Father's Ford Pinto. We was no Romero & Juliet & she was sure no looker— but we got sticky all the same as Ungin's do

Then. Wen she went & broke up w/ me on the first day of summer vacation, I was awful hartbroken. Lovesick, they call that

I spent a lot time alone that summer of '84. C, I'd been alone near evry summer befor that, but this was a new alone. It was an alone after having known the pleazure of a woman. That make sents? That first hartbrake makes a *new* alone that's angrier & fuller of piss & vinegur.

So, I got to working a job. A job ceemed to have helped Donnie with his angers and it sure helped ma with here deemons of alkehall. So I scort me this gig mowing lawns. This local fella gave me a mower & a blower & told me to cut these big comersal propertys like the church & the dollar house & this big offiss park for dentysts & lawyers. It was a lot of grass & lot of hard work, specially in the middle of the Alabama summer & the pay was shit to; but, I was fond of the guy I worked for. His name was Mr. Hearst. Mr. Hearst used to call me 'sir' & he always paid me on time. A man don't never forget a nother man like that

Mr. Hearst trimmed trees at all them places that I mowed & sumtimes he'd talk to me about football or movies & 1ce, he gave me his son's gitar on acount his son wasn't behaving rite & he rekond his son didn't diserve no gitar no more

I tell U, baby, I took to that gitar like it was my new lover. Played that sucker all nite long wile I drunk up bottles of wiskey that Donnie brung in from the city on his weekly visits.

I look back at that summer of '84 and baby, I thote I was reelly hurting

I thote I new pain. But that wasn't real hurt. In truth, thems was probably sum of the best days I had in this hear life. The sun-burny fool I was; mowing lawns by day & by nite, picking my fingers bloody trying to learn me sum Rebel rock off an AM radio. All the wiles, yearning for an ugly girl watwhomst I never kwite loved to begins with

I lernt me two inportant discoveries doring this lost summer

1stly, I lernt that I culd not sing. Not 1 damm note

2dly: I learnt that If I was skunk drunk. All cross-eyed & stumble-hammered—& I tried using my mindsnake; the biteback wasn't so bad. It's kinda like how they used to give wiskey to sivil war soldiers wen they had to cut off their gangrinus legs. I gess alkhillhawl… alcoehawl… alckehole… is a natral pain-killer cause it killed the rite shit out of the biteback

Wen I was drunk off my ass, I culd fling darts into my dart board. Perfect bullseyes even. 1 after a nother and it sure hurt the next day, but when I was doin it I didnt feel nuffing.

Booze, I lernt, made me unstoppable— or at least it made it EZer to work the snake coming out of my head

X

Eventually came a day wen they kicked me out of hischool & not w/ no diploma neether.

I was 18 years a wild animal & Anjel Baby I didn't care not 1 shoe string for Bethlahem, Alabama

So I pooled sum of Mr. Hearst lawn mowing monie w/ sum of my vending macheen heist monie, & I bot me a ticket to Calerfornya. Nows, I culd lie & say I was inchrested in surfing, or chasing sum music dream, but Anjle Baby U no dam well wat brot me to Calerfornya. There were pretty girls out there & unlike the pretty girls in New York or Dallas, the pretty girls in Calerfornya wuld give all ther sweet loving to the uglyest little fella on the planet so long as that little fella culd string together two chords on a gitar

At least that was how the movies & the tv made it seem.

I don't ritely no how I ended up in El Centro, but El Centro was where the bus let me off & El Centro was where I staiyed. Little shitheel town on the border to old Mexico. Nothing much there but brown sand and hiways

I got off that bus expecting bare titties & a beech party; but about all's I found was a month-to-month leece on a dingy apartment above a motorsykle bar

My new home smelt like motorsykle man piss & it sounded like ther angry street macheens. I all to kwikly disckovred that bikers make for real shit naybors; Always fiteing in the streets & blasting ther jet engines. I used to lie awake on my floor matriss & I wuld fantasize about killing the biker men downstairs. It'd be almost like a seen U'd wat C in a movie. I'd go down to the bar & ask those fellas real nice to kwiet down, & they'd say sumthing tuff, & I'd say sumthing tuff, & then they'd take out a gun, & BOOM I'd start making ther heads pop with my sychic powers, or, make them stab theyselves w/ ther own nives. That sort of thing

Corss, my mindsnake wasn't poweful enuff for sumthin like that. Those was just the angry dreams of a yung fool in a strange new place

And a strange new place its was, anjel baby. A strange new place it was

All them movies I had grown up with— and all them songs on the radio— I had thote Calerfornya wuld be 1 non-stop origie of free sex, drugs & rock & roll; that the parties would be as easy to find as a mac docunlds. But I never did find a party. Or an easy lady. Or drugs. Or even a frend for that madder; I never even found the beech. To my surprise it turned out El Centro was a dammt landlokt city in the middle of the dessert and it was damm near 2 hours to the beech

W/ rent over my hed & not a damm thing to do, I had to take a dayjob. I ended up w/ a broke bastard kind of gig, the kind where they hire anybody w/ two eyes & ten fingers. It was at this disstrrebubewshon center that emported premade sinks, shitters & bathtubs from Mexico—& shit, them boxes was heavy. Work started at 5 in the goddam morning & didn't end until 1 PM.

Baby, that potty factory worked me like the ugly dog I was. But it put cash in my pocket. And wen I got off work, I'd set out on my conkwest for good Calyfornnya times. I started by making myself hansome. I showered (with soap), put on them bell bottom jeans & back then I had me a silk shirt with blue flowers on it & I bot me some colon to match the way I thote it shuld smell.

1ce I was rite pretty & flowery smellin, I went out hounding for trim. I must have visited evry bar in El Centro. Wern't too many of them; just a few sports tavirns and cannedtinas, and I used to go to these places & sit alone at the bar & nurse shots of wiskey. I'd make myself look real sad. C, that's wat guys did at the start of movies & tv shows. A guy sits there looking sad & the woman in the show comes & tells the guy how lonely & sad he looks & then the loving gets started

But the real world didn't seem a work that way. No m'am. Not 1 miss or mam or senorita never told me how lonely or sad I looked & I always walked home alone. On a good nite I'd maybe flip up a few skirts, but, never 1ce did a skirt fly off up at my apartment. Maybe the pretty girls of the world are all the real thote-reading sikiks & they saw me there at the bar & they knew I was just little eggboy from Bethlahem; playing dress up as somebody I wasn't

I never did get me a Califyornya girl

X

Humping boxes at that potty factory took years off my spine, I tell U wat. I took to walking round a lot. It made the pain easyer & it felt better than lieing at home & wishing death on the motobikers downstares

I'd walk round this shit town I'd come to & wunder who I was supposed to be egzakly. I got to deciding that Jesus, or whoever, had given me a special gift in the form of this mind snake & I was skwandering it by humping shitters 8 hours a day. C, I needed to turn my mindsnake into a monie making operation & not no vending macheene monie neether. Real money

$$$.

C now, my first thote was I culd be a majician, theys proally make lots of money, rite? But this hear idea fell apart on acount Im terryfied of crowds &, well, I'd probibly need an hour of tricks to keep peeple sadisfied & just using the snake for ten seconds gave me a feeling like I was getting a lowbottleme by saskwatch. So—a carear as a majician was not in the cards.

My next thote was stealing. I meen, I thote of this before, but I starting thinking about it harder. There was this 1 idea I had; where I'd go to a gas station & wen the cash register opent, I'd make all the monie fly out into my pocket. That, or maybe I culd fool an ATM the way I fooled a sodypop macheen. These ideas was fine, but, theys was just 1 extra step above robbry. Now, Im no law a biting citizen, but Im no smooth crimnal neether—first I had to be real drunk to do anything w/ the snake & it wern't gonna be easy running from cops with a belly filt of wiskey. And if I gots cot, who was to say they wuldn't put me in sum kind of CIA zoo for weerdos w/ supper powers. So—a crimnal I was not neether.

So's just wen I was plump out of ideas I was struck w/, a wadya call it, an et piffany. As if it com down from on hi

It happent in 1 moment

Baby, U know, there's these little moments that go on to define Ur life & U look back on 'em & it makes U feel stupid that sumthing so itty-bitty-tiny up & changed who U was supposed to be in this world. Who U spent it with. How U died. My stupid itty-bitty-tiny moment happent in a game of snooker

There was this 1 day; I was bored & my back was hurt to shit from shitter humping & I was tired of being a broke bastard & I had this nasty dieper rash between my legs from walking round so damm much. So, I desided to go to the closest bar to my home bed & I finally tried out that biker bar 1 story down the fire escape. It was a rainy Wensday afternoon, so there wern't so many folks round; only the old fart bikers. With nothing better to do, I drank to much wiskey w/ these old dogs wile theys told me ther stories about how tuff they used to be

1 of the old timers, he looked like Santa's letherdaddy cousin, he asked me to play a game of pool w/ him on this ratty old table & I indulged this hear feller in a round of snooker for a bet of 5 dollar$ of pocket cash

Now. To my shock, this fat old biker may have, in fact, been the greatest pool player ever known by mankind. Straight from braking, he was kickin' my ass; he called every shot & sank damm near all his balls on 1 turn

Now, on my first turn, I called thirteen for the corner pocket. I shot the cue ball for the ornje stripey & the fool I was, I shot to hard. The 13 sank & the cue ball hit that edge & what was about to fall in w/ it (meaning I'd lose the game). Now, rite there at that last second befor sure & total defeat— I had me this knee-jerk reeaction, I shot out my mindsnake & steadied the cue ball from falling in

Saved me the cueball & saved me from losing (rite then at least)

The old biker said I'd got lucky, but, Anjle Baby, that fella didn't now the haff of it. That white ball gave me 1 brite idea

I went on to lose that game of snooker, & lose them 5 dollar$, but I knew I had me a fortune comin

X

I had to leeve behind my gitar. My matriss to. & It was long, hot journey to do by bus, but I got to Las Vegas round sunset the very next nite & Anjle Baby I don't got to tell U; it looked like it did in all them movies. All thems blinking lites & pritty shiny peeple. All thems giant sexy words written in elecktrisity and big litebulbs. All that so-muchedness; Gold & limozines & feathered up boobys rite on the street. I swear I culd smell monie on all that dry air

I member hearing that casino song for the first time, poring out from those big old doors onto the street; ten thousand jingling slot mashines; and I tellya, a choir of anjles culdn't make a sound so beautiful

Fresh off the bus, I didn't have enuff monie for a hotel, hell, I didn't even have me a change of close. Alls I had me was a flower shirt, some shoes, haff a sikik power & seven bucks cash in the pocket of my bell bottoms

I spent two of them dollars on a pint of vodka from a mini-mart. Chugged it the alley to get my mindsnake nice & luce. Then I took my fiver to the closest casino I culd get it to on foot; it was this little joint called the Red Dragon. Trashy place. I member they had a big Chinese food buffet & ain't nobody was eatin it cause the food lookt rite nasty. There was this big gold dragon on the ceiling, that fella there had paper fire coming out of his mouth & all those little china donut gold coins falling off his belly. I member lookin at that dragon & thinking that fella there was about to be me! $$$

So's I bot me a 5 dollar chip, a little plastic disk, green w/ black checkers on the rim, and baby, that chip there was my ticket to the world. I wandered up to the rulette tables; found me 1 full of a bunch of old ladies & I put my 5 dollars on black. Yes mam. A tiny fella in a bow tie said *no more bets* & he spun the weel. Then, I reelly focused, I took the mindsnake out & flopped it there onto the rulette table & I followt & followt that little white perl & wen it slowed, & it was just about to jump onto red, I reeched out & I knicked it from a 1 to 13; froms red to black

Alls it took was a little nudge. Maybe if U new wat I was doing U culda Cn it, but, for all the other gamblers, & more importantly, the guy running the weel, it looked like nothing more than a bounce, tinier than a bell bobbling 'round a baby lambs neck

The little bowtie man told me congrajulasions & he tossed me 2 5 dollar chips. That's what U call a 100 persent return invessment

Anjle Baby, as of that moment, I was never a poor man not never again

X

I think wat made me special from most folks, trulee yunike, was wenever I lost time I made monie. Not a lot of folks can say that

The memry round that first nite on the weel is kinda like that. All those little keepysake moments are drowned in the licker; long island ice T's to be specific, complimentree from a pretty watress in black seakwin dress

I lost 2 days & 2 nites to the licker when I first came to Vegas

All's I do member is waking up in another casino's hotel, my hed in the toilet & my brane drier than the mohave dessert. But, wen I stumbled up & opened the door to my rented bedroom, there upon my sheets was nothng but cash$. Cash in bags. Cash in popcorn buckets. More cash than I culd have ever dremt of in my lifetime 2ce over. All won by a chasing perls with a snake from a drunk fellers brain

1st thing I did was go lie down & sleep in it

X

I tell U wat; I herd this story not so long ago. These guys a few tables over from me at the Palm Grande were talking about this sichological study. C, these colledge eggheads took a rat, an ordynary street rat & they gave this rat a button & U C, this rat hear got cheeze evry time he pushed this button, & so wat do U think that rat did? He just sat there pushing that cheeze button all damm day long until he was the size of a dang racooon. They said that rat got depreshion. I didn't even now a rat culd get depreshion

That story there made me think a bout about me, specially my Unger me in those early Vegas days. C, that colledge rat got hisself a cheeze button but Urs trulee had a monie button—& wen U grow up on dirt floors & Sundy dinner from the church's tin-can donation box, it's not easy to stop pushing the monie button

If I had to gess, I'd say I made, oh, about 300000 dollars over my first week in Vegas. Therebouts. It was easy. Chasing marbles on the weel. I'd drink & I'd win & I'd drink & I'd win & I'd drink & I'd win until the bitebacks got so bad I'd pass out rite there at the table. That or get thron out on the street on acount I was drunker than peepee le pew

I got robbed 1 nite wen I passed out w/ all my cash in a hotel elevator. They must have made off with a few 1000 bucks from my pockets. Didn't matter tho. I just kept putting monie on black & nocking the marbles where they needed to go. It was just that easy.

& for a good long, long time that was my life. Pressing down on a button until the sleep found me

ventully I bot myself a weekly stay in the shittiest motel off the strip & I got me myself a rootine. I'd wake up, usually round 3 or 4 in the afternoon. Maybe go for a walk. Maybe have a donut or a coffee from the incontinental brekfast. Then I'd choose me a casino

I'd jack arond first; eat the boofet, play cards for fun or shoot the shit w/ the pretty watresses, sumtimes I tried figuring out how to cheat the slot masheens, but, slots are a whole lot more complercated than vending masheens on acount they got microchips & I never did kwite get it figured how to cheat no computer microchip

—but without fail, by nitefall, I was sure to have returned to my red & black checker prison weel, where it was my job to drink licker & bounce the perls to the black. On & on & on t'il there was no more membering to be done

Jesus Christ, minus the days I was lying dead, snakebit & hungover —that was evry day. I'd go home w/ monies busting out the seams of a plastic take out bag. Sum days were 72 hours long and sum days never even got started. Time past me by mezered in booze and bags of cash. Not hours. Or minutes. Or days. Just green green money

I tell U Anjle Baby, sumware along the way I became a millyonair and didn't not even know it. I got bored & fat & a special kind of lonesum. Started spending money just to feel sumething. Kinda had to spend it on a count I didnt have no more room in my motel to store it all. The drawer. The closet. The underside of the bed, they was all over run with cash bags. So Id piss monie away on clothes & watches—boots— special hundred year old Scotch from scotsland. Snakeskin hats & jackets. Custom fit suits.

Japnese Boomboxes & cigars w/ gold labels. Haff of these hear purcheyses went undrank, unworn or unsmoked. They just hung round my motel room like treasure in a mummys toom

X

I bot my first hooker at the end of my 2nd week in Vegas. Erly erly on. Her name was Monica. Picked her rite up off the sidewalk. U'd think a hookers name wuld be like roxie or sumthin, but, no, she was Monica. She came cheap & she looked funny in brite lite. She didn't kiss me neether. Which I didn't like. Cause Im awful fond of kissing. Kissing makes a man feel beloved

I learned early on that it takes a lot of monie to buy good fake luv (the kind that comes w/ the kissin). So's I slowly spent more & more on nitegirls until I ended up w/ a hi dollar hore habit near as expensive as any coke addickshun

I paid these womens for the bedroom, sure, but, I was fond of the girls who'd pretend to be my girly-frend. They'd go walking w/ me or sit w/ me wile I played slots or go swimming in the motel swimming pool. Sumtimes I'd dress 'em up like dollies & take them to dinner sumplace nice w/ bubbly & violins & a waiter who called me 'sir' like Mr. Hearst used to.

But—I always had to pay them extra for all that pretending—& wen the ugly lie of the morning come, they'd look at me the way I looked at my rulette table

All those rotten months, I was a cheeze button for hookers, & Anjle Baby, wen U added up all them hours, the perls they was chasing wasn't paying out neer as good

X

Life can sour into a rite ugly effair, &, then, out the blue, it's bewtyful again. I gess life is kinda like gambling in that way. Say what U want about Jesus having a plan for U, it's all just bullshit how them cards get stacked

It was summer, and baby I was one swetty, miserable millyonair with a pickled brain. I member walking arond the strip and thinking about taking my own life

1 day, I was in a fowl mood & just about fed up w/ life & all the money & hores, & then, out from the storm clouds came U; Anjle Baby from Las Vegas. Hear in a city of sun-dried lizard womens; I found U, this long body lollipop girl, w/ big old feet, & strawbry blonde hair, & legs as long as route 66. U was hardly a day over fifteen, asking for lucies outside the sevens'leven wen I was heading in to get me sum hangover cola pop

U asked me to sell U a sigret & I said I was a gentleman so's I'd buy U a whole pack; watever brand U fancied

I bot U Virgina slims & a sixer of wino coolers to boot.

Wen U struck up that first sigret, U told me U liked my snake skin hat. I told U it was so new so U'd better be careful; if U got to close it mite bite U. U smiled & that's when I first new u was gonna be my furever girlie

X

I gess we had that crazy kind of luv. Didn't we? We just culdn't be seprated. Didn't matter how mad Ur daddy was; U loved me crazy & I loved U back crazy dubble. It feels like U & me lived in Vegas for sumthing like 10000 years, wen in truth it was only but a few mear months

It didn't take long for U to leave Ur folks & come stay w/ me in my treasure nest

We lived inside a dreem; U, me & all our pet cocaroches in our crusty motel room off the strip. I close my eyes & I can still C the booger green mold in the hot tub, the hart shaped bed w/ majic finger box & all those stacks of styrofome clamshells scattered about the shag carpet

U used to bleed me dry eating all them candy bars out of the mini-fridge. U were a kid then, I gess & I was still halfway a kid. But U still introdooced me to all those crazy pills & smokables. I'd get home from working the weel & then U'd take me outerspace w/ sum majic desert root

U didn't care how the monie worked back then. U'd ask how I win so dang much & I'd just tell U: baby, Im just lucky & Ur my proof of sutch a fact

Tell U wat, if I had the supper power of time travel instedd of telekeenezis, I'd go back to those doggie days on our hart shaped bed; eating pizza & burnt stake from clamshells. Renting porno movies. Doin' it on piles of money

U mite hate me now, but U'll always be my Anjle Baby. Always my crazy luv. Given the choice; I'd go back to our wildest days 'fore I'd go to heven

X

Corss there came that day in Vegas. That bad day. U never did get the whole piture

C, now. I was dum, but I wasn't no dum-dum. I new U culdn't just win over & over again at the same table at the same place. So I did my best to deversify; never win to much in 1 seat, 1 table, 1 place. But U C, even w/ all that work to keep movin; I was still the 1 in a millyon dedycated gamblers who was running on a profet instedd of a loss & subody was bound to notiss eventally

It was a Sundy in the ded heat at the end of agust. I went to The King Arther on the strip; the platnum armor room. Proababbly Round 3 AM it was. I drank my majic juice. I put 800 on black & then bam; a pair of these tuxedo'd Frankenstein's picked me up by either arm & polightely, but firmly, rekwested I join them in the back of the house

They carried me to a little locker room w/ drains on the floor & Baby, those boys did ther damdest to crack evry bone in my body

I just member sitting there, getting kicked round like a socker ball & wishing I culd use my powers to defend myself. But, using powers took to much focus. My mindsnake just flopped round w/ the rest of me like a big old hotdog weener

Rite sudden, wen they was done beating me, this little man came in. Fella was white haired & ainshent. He kinda looked like Mr. Monoply wat from the bordgame. He drug this metal chair w/ him & it made this real loud screeching sound, on & on he went, guy must have walked thirty feet scratching the floor. Wen he got rite up next to me he set the chair up & sat down

Then this little fella leant in & he told me all of 2 words; "Skip town" & Baby, I told him all of 2 words back. yes and sir

X

The scare I must have gave U, sweet child; wen I got back to the motel all covered in bruises & blood & sum of my own piss. I tolds U bad men were after me & we needed to go N-O-W!

I gave U a duffel bag of cash & told U to go buy us a car. Any car U'd like, & sure as shit U came back from the x-otic deeler lot with a vintage Desodo Convertyble; hot pink with black lepard spots

We left our city of Vegas in a toy car packed to the brim w/ paper monie & sparkly tressure. I member writhing arond on our brand new back seats using wads of cash & hi end panties to stop the bleeding on my varUs wounds

U just had Ur learning permit then. U wern't even supposed to be driving. Hell, U cried the whole way to Texas

X

I suppose it was that southbound drawl of the hiway wat took us to our little beech house in Gulf Hills, Missppi

I never thote we'd stick round this old place so long. All these years, I always thote I'd get found out by the casinos &, well, I'd get beet to a pulp again & we'd have to flee 1ce more into the nite for Atlanic City or sum such place

But I never did get run off. Maybe the casino security round Missippi ain't so sophisticated as Vegas or maybe I got to smart at my cheatin'.

C, I had me a sistem all these years down hear, I got real good at making myself look like a loser. That was always my kamUflajj… camouflojj… *camo*… Make 'em think Im the lowdest, unluckyest loser these peeple had ever Cn & making it look like that was an easy on acount I'd already been a lifelong lozer

I came into these hear Missippi casinos in the early afternoon wen it was slow & I came wearing all my shiny screaming raddlesnake scales & I swore loud, & I ordered lots & lots of drinks & I smacked the watresses rear ends & I played buddy buddy w/ the floor manejers. I made damm sure all eyes were on me, & honey, wile them eyes were on me: I lost. I burned monie like I was using it to keep warm in a blizzard. I'd feed slot machines ten thousand dollars. I'd leave 100 dollar chips behind at the table. I'd have me a 19 in a hi-steakes game of blackjack & I'd deemand the dealer to hit me. Yes M'am, & then, by nite, I made my winnings in the shadows. I'd come in all kwyet-like in aviator shades & a big baggie hoodie. I'd take my biznes to the most crowded rulette table I culd find, &, in all that hoolaballoo, I'd get to chasing perls w/ a snake. Pushing my cheeze button if U will. Sure shooting, little by little, I stuffed my pockets w/ all the monie I'd lost that day & then sum, & then sum, & then sum

This was my process. My day job. Was for damm near a decade & change

Sumtimes, wen the drives were long & hauling all that paper cash got tedius, I'd think about getting a real job—like the way I used to mow lawns or hump potties

I thote maybe I culd open a chiken finger restorant or a tiddy bar or, maybe a DJ business. Maybe I culd breed jerman sheperds or go do sum learning at a collage. Buy a airplane and teach peeple to skydive. Sumthing neat like that— a cool dude job, but shit, Anjle Baby, a job wuld have killed my very soul

C, there's work & then there's cheating & even the most miserable grift is always gonna make for a better paycheck than any honest J-O-B

X

So... now.

It's 4AM as I doodle this hear sewiside note on pen & yellow paper. Ain't kwite time to go yet. Im nervos

The revolvers loded & I gived a goodbi kiss to the last photo I got with me, Donnie & Ma' all in it. Im hear on our balcny w/ a cup of irish coffee, watching the osean slobber at the nite. I watch the black sea & I wunder wat will happen to the world wen it gets away from me.

U no I always thote I'd become a surfer. Maybe buy a boat. We never did that did we? I member that long bus ride as a yung man bound for calyfornya. The way I wanted to see the ocean. Now, I'm Livin' rite by the sea. Been here for years. Got more monie than god & I ain't ever bot no damm boat. Makes me feel a fool. Where did the time go? Who took it all from me?

X

I get angery thinking about all those years behind me that dont even feel much like years at all. All those months stolen by the weel & the snake. It's a pityfull creature I've become sliding cash arond these Missippi casinos

I cant give U no son. I cant hardly reed or rite. Cant hardly stand on my own 2 feet. All I do is hurt & cheat & drink & hurt & cheat & hurt & drive 7 hours & sleep for 3 days strate & wake up & hurt & drink & cheet

Feels like yesterday we were meeting at a sevensleven. Now U got Ur city frends & Ur weekends in Miami & I got my 12 car grage & I got my big hallway of gitars I don't even play no more & all this big old house does is echo emtty sound

I look at myself in the mirror; all carved up by these years like sum kind of Jack O Lantern left over at XMAS. My skin's yellow & all the hair run off the top of my hed. Spine's broke. Liver's fucked &, baby, I got a 4 foot indvisble tentcle coming out of my forhead & I can feel it dyin. This power wasn't good for my constitootion. It scrambled up my brane meat like a cancer. The power is leevin and its takin me with it. & aint No doctor's gonna fix this old cheeze rat. I hurt. I hurt bad. It's all those years of bitebacks & hard licker. I got angry bees in my skull & trane whistles in my ears & my thotes don't make sense. I feel damm near 80s years old & can only member about 3 things

X

U no pain has it's way of eating joy up like a fat kid in a pillow case full of snikkers. Pain just can't help itself & I never culd help myself from driving down to a casino & putting more pain inside me. Pain goppled up these missippi years & pain gobbled up all the luv I was supposed to be bringing home to U. My betroved

I wish I'd been kinder to U, Anjle Baby. I wish I hadn't put my pain into U. All that yellin and screamin

I hope that wen U look back on the life I gaved U, U find that our luv was, at a bear minemom, always servicyble. U needed for nuffing. Can't say I didn't take U places. Can't say I didn't listen to U &, hey, I never laid a finger on U. How about that? I was a man who never hit his woman. Not me. U sure dared me. U sure said sum dumb shit that warrented a kwick smack on the chin, but, I hit the walls in Ur stead

I hope U keep this old house on the beech & I hope U keep those holes I made in the walls. I hope U look at them & U member each time I hit our house instedd of hitting U.

It's what I leave U w/, them emty holes in the drywall

I don't care wat Ur fancy pants therapist says; U can never stop loving me & even wen the sun itself blows up, the past will still be the past & we'll always be there; lovers on a hart shaped bed in Las Vegas

X

That last part was supposed to be the last part

But I watched sum TV & then the morning sun come round. I wasn't ready to die. Not in the dark & not on no emtty stomach neether

So's I desided to go for 1 last ride round 8 AM. Make my peace w/ this gnarly old planet. U was sleeping. So I put a kiss on U. Consider that my tru & tru final goodby

X

…On the ride out of town I saw sum teenaged kid mowing lawns & I wundered to myself if maybe that boy there had got hisself any secret majic powers like I do…

I traveled out west to the Palm Grande where I done had myself a 10AM stake & I ordered it well done the way I like it w/ curly fries, sodypop & a goddammt bannanna split w/ two scoops of chocolett & no vaniller

After my last meal, I went up to the Palm Grande's game floor manejer & I said Mister; I need to show U wat I got in the parking lot. C, Anjle Baby, I took the Humvee out w/ me today on acount it was the only car that culd wat fit all our cash monie.

I brot the payload w/ me. Evry damm dollar we have. I showed that floor manejer a cash loaded Humvee & I said to him, I says: *Mister, I don't got long to live; I want to put it all on black. The keys to*

Man said *Yes sir*

He had to have sum of his back of the house boys count it all, but wen they was done, manejer com up & put a special gold chip in my hand. *Pony up,* he said to me.

Now, I took that chip direct to my rulette weel where I was gonna chase my last perl.

Wasn't a soul there. Just me & the little Navajo boy who wat spun the weel. Fella gave me a big smile as I set that chip on black; Evry dollar I evr stole, all my illgottme ganes down for 1 last ride. Dubble or nothin

& baby, that boy spun & that weel clicker clackered & befor I set the snake out for a chase, I made me a last minit decision

I let that perl run all its own. No majic. No mindsnake, no cheat

— I sat back simple & done watched— In truth, it reminded me of the way me & Donnie used to throe rocks at cars on the interstate. Set sumthing lose. Let it free. & I was free. I didnt hurt neether. I was just a good ol boy watching an honest rock fly

& Round & round the white perl went like the sun making its wayround the earth to make the years. Like jonny in his star ship cruzin round the unyverse devine

& Wen the weel came to a slow, that there marble hobbled on the gold line between 1 & 13; & for the first time in a good, long, long time, I finely membered wat it ment to be lucky

WOMAN IN CHAIR FILM

I have been sent to New York City to broker the exchange of a high-value VHS tape.

—

At twenty-two hundred hours local time, I arrive in Manhattan via a flight called GA712; an airbus direct from London.

A tunnel discharges me to a brightly lit, crowded pavilion of benches and snack vendors. This place is John F. Kennedy airport; a place they named for a man they shot in the head on live television. Here, in this dead man's namesake, are wailing babies, fat men eating hamburgers from paper wrappers, and smooth-chinned businessmen who bark orders on their gray brick cellular phones.

A PA system plays *Jingle Bell Rock*.

I put on my sunglasses and head for customs.

—

It is almost 0000 hours by the time I get my passport stamped.

I exit onto a train platform, now. This place too is occupied by the crowds of the blue-jean-and-baseball-hat Americans. Some flash me overly earnest smiles. Why? I don't know. There's something so desperate about these people. That obligation to smile. That neediness for joy. Approval.

Victory. The American is never satisfied. Always hungry: for friends, for food, for time. Money. Entertainment.

A light snow falls on me; it dusts my shoulders where I stand beside the tracks with heels upon the yellow line.

I look up as I await the train. The sky is without stars in this corner of the world. I see are the spires of glass block buildings and, above them, twinkling helicopters or airplanes swimming in a gray candle smoke.

They had warned me the city of New York smells of rats and stale urine and rotten vegetables; it appears these warnings were correct.

—

After a transfer, I find myself on one of the famous New York subway train cars. Orange chairs like something from an asylum, graffiti carvings, and flickering lights. Advertisements.

I travel below the earth in black grime tunnels on a screeching metal monstrosity. At every stop more people board. Tourists. Locals. Vagrants. Children. The train becomes so congested I worry that I will suffocate. Beside me, a pair of teenagers wrestle; opposite me, an old couple loudly argue in Chinese. To my cat's eye corner, a woman exposes herself in an outfit of torn leather underwear, her face full of thumbtacks and safety pins.

Halfway through the ride, a man who smells of armpits enters our car. He plays a broken violin; he walks the crowded aisle expecting pocket change. When people give him their quarters and dimes he tells them: *Merry Christmas*.

I keep my head down. I wear headphones and play my tapes of electronic jazz. I close my eyes and pretend I do not smell the rats and urine and that unique American flesh stink of fried milk bowels and cheap perfume. I think of my house beside the forest in my home country. I think of my mission here, and the tape I have been sent to retrieve.

—

I serve as the left hand of a man known to most simply as Starikova. He is my Pakhan— *my boss.* I belong to him.

Once, decades ago, he was what an American calls a soldier of fortune, but he found this work much too dangerous, and instead became a smuggler. He dedicated the early eighties to importing contraband niceties from Kazakhstan into Novosibirsk. Such things like chocolates. Coffees. Perfumes. Televisions.

Along the way he realized a special skill for film distribution.

Before the fall of the Soviet Union, Starikova was known as *Novosibirsk's Movie King.* He smuggled in films in a myriad of formats and realized methods for their mass duplication, or *pirating* as the Americans call it. Quickly he found himself a crime boss of sorts with his large network of shops and sellers, not just in Novosibirsk, but in St. Petersburg and Moscow too, as well as all the small towns along his smuggler's road at the border.

His best selling items were home media players. Cheap VHS and Betamax systems constructed by a bootleg factory in India. Half of these machines didn't even work, but people still paid top dollar for them; because people love movies. Don't they? It's a simple universal constant and it was one Starikova understood well. He amassed a fortune simply by duplicating little black boxes with Hollywood movies on the tape: *popcorn flicks* and s*ummertime blockbusters* with Tom Cruise or Val Kilmer and big explosions. Alien invasion movies. Cowboy movies. Movies about ghosts or teenagers living college wetdream.

By the time the Berlin Wall fell, Pakhan Starikova found the opportunity to expand his empire and invested in more legitimate filmmaking operations. Now he launders his fortunes through a company called Shedevry Kino. Shedevry Kino imports movies and home entertainment systems legally and distributes them along his existing networks, but by no means does his entire organization operate within the confines of the law.

In more recent years, Pakhan Starikova's most fortuitous venture, and perhaps his most personal obsession too, is pornography. If Starikova was once the movie king of Novosibirsk, today he would be better suited for the title of *Porno King of Novosibirsk.*

Not only does he import *adult films* (as Americans call them) but he funds their production and export. He operates a studio in Novosibirsk out of his own home and also runs a nearby discotheque, a mere front to launder his money and entice young women to appear in his movies.

It is another universal constant Starikov seems to have recognized; that there is money to be made on the world's stranger tastes; on men's most perverse fantasies and darkest desires.

I wish I could unsee some of the things I have seen. Some of the films he has made, those which I have helped in the facilitation of creating. Starikova is thought by any decent man to be a cancer, but I am the left hand of this cancer. I have sold my soul for the fruits born of his dirty work and I will serve this man until my dying breath.

—

It is deeper into the night when I emerge into the subway exit tunnels; now I am in central Manhattan. Here, lurking among the crowds, I walk a long hallway of white tile basked in electric green light. It reminds me of a public shower. The walls are occasionally plastered with movie posters that have been defaced with permanent markers; their Hollywood stars now bear faces of death with blacked out eyes and slurs written across their foreheads.

Above me, I hear the growl of more yellow taxis and the howling of street lunatics.

—

The topside streets do not smell any better than the tubes. I turn up the volume on my headphones and maneuver through more destitute homeless and pleading beggars. Stray dogs eat at snow-covered hills of garbage bags. The yellow taxi cabs drive too fast on streets of black ice slime. Behind black windows, rich people eat steak and drink red wine.

Whenever business takes me to the United States, I only bring a single backpack. This is so I do not have much to lose in the event of a theft. My bag contains a hygiene kit, three pairs of underpants, three pairs of socks and three undershirts. I wear the same outfit for the days that I am here. I wear America-style blue jeans and a sharp-collared cowboy shirt. I have a leather duster with broad padded shoulders and cape that extends to my ankles. This outfit is to make me appear like Schwarzenegger's Terminator. I do this so street gangs do not try to domineer me. I complete this appearance with shield sunglasses; a large visor that covers the top half of my face. I wear these glasses at all times, even at night, so prospective combatants cannot predict my vision.

As I walk through a more abandoned area, I lower the music on my headphones so I might better hear a surprise attack.

"Hey Mister Shades! Mister Shades!"

Suddenly, a black boy jumps into my direct path. An overgrown child with snotty nose and a bright orange snowcap. He is lucky I do not break his snotty nose. He waves a box of eight-tracks. He calls me *Mister Shades* again and tries to sell me some of his wares of black boy music. He tells me they would make a good Christmas present for my sweetheart. I walk past him, and he readily moves on to the next stranger.

I do not respect this boy, but I am empathetic of his trade.

This is how I got my start, twelve long years ago.

There was once a time when I drank water from the storm drains and ate food from the refuse bins. I was once a boy of the alleyways, selling whatever I could find to get by.

I came under the employ of Starikova when I was but thirteen years old. Not directly. I worked for one of his underbosses who used young boys for general labor. I was paid next to nothing to work tape copying machines and move boxes about a warehouse. Simple work fit for an idiot, but I did it well, and held onto this job because the alternative was freezing in the streets.

My true calling was revealed in a few years time, when I was a teenager. A competitor pirate organization came to Novosibirsk and because I figured myself tough, I volunteered for retaliatory operations. These were simple jobs initially, like running rival street kids off our corners, but soon I was shutting down competitors by breaking their duplication machines with a baseball bat. Later I burned trucks and cut off the fingers of shop owners who refused to sell our products.

My ruthless efforts did not go unnoticed or unrewarded.

By the time I was a man, I was a close associate of Pakhan Starikova; a minion of the underground porn king of Novosibirsk. I am officially paid as a security officer for his film studio, a job which primarily consists of beating actresses who wish to exit their contracts with Shedevry Kino. This, or making certain objectors to his business— *disappear.*

Now, I have become the left hand of the boss himself. *His body man* as they might say in an American movie, with my own room inside his palace compound. I stand over him in his daily meetings, I drive him to and fro. I am the man's shadow, only leaving when I am assigned to handle his most delicate missions. Such as this.

I believe he regards me as a close personal friend, though these are feelings I do not reciprocate.

Starikova was once a serious man. But old age has made him an eccentric fool. He is a small, portly, snickering drunk. He has the mind of a child: prone to tantrums and random acts of cruelty. He has the diet of a child as well: American foods, like can-spray cheese and candy milk cereals. In spite of his portly shape he often dresses in leather body garments like those worn by Michael Jackson or Eddie Murphy's *Raw*.

I believe it was the movies; he watched too many and they melted his mind. Gave him cavities of the brain. Now his life is an endless cycle of vodka, pornography and bullying the unlucky girls he calls his girlfriends.

I would enjoy nothing more than to see Starikova disemboweled; but he is the reason I do not drink from storm drains or forage my meals from dumpsters. He is the reason I am not that boy hustling eight tracks from the alleyways. I am Starikova's dog and I am his loyal dog.

—

Shedevry Kino has provided me lodging with private bed and kitchen. This is by request, as I do not trust American restaurants and their menus consisting of cheese and cola. I visit a dank and disheveled supermarket near my final destination, a bodega they call this; here I collect my meal provisions for this trip.

A black cat wanders the aisles freely to eat mice and cockroaches. It nuzzles against my ankles before I kick it away.

I purchase tinned salmon, cabbage, parsley, rice and potatoes; enough food for three days. The cashier tries to make conversation with me before I direct my finger to my headphones.

—

I check in to a brand name lodge near Times Square. The lobby is disguised to seem as though it were a luxury hotel, but no one knows a bootleg better than I do. This is a den of bed bugs for tourists from Iowa. At the main entrance a hollowed out piano sits beside an overly decorated Christmas Tree of plastic branches and bulbs that flash in primary colors.

I must remove my headphones to speak with a man at a tinsel-wrapped check-in desk.

The man here, behind a computer, is black skinned. He is elderly. He wears a humiliating velvet fez and an admiral jacket with cheap yellow epaulets. In his elaborate uniform he appears to me like a disgraced warlord, awaiting execution. A golden name tag reads Tahir.

Tahir is uncomfortable with his computer. His eyes seem diseased. They are red and yellow. He asks me if I'm checking in.

"*Shedevry Kino,*" I say to him, firmly.

"For check-in?" He struggles with the computer. "Shuh-Dovery."

"*Shedevry Kino,*" I correct him.

"Yes, yes— Say it for me one more time?"

"*Shedevry Kino.*"

English is not his first language. I can hear it on his tongue. I can hear his hatred. His fatigue. He hates this language like I do; pig language of devils who eat fried lard.

A man half his age, pudgy Germanic in a clip-on tie, passes behind him.

He moos like a cow, "Hey, Tahir, buddy—George had to run home, okay? He's got a tummy bug or something. So, can you go retrieve the luggage carts off eight and six?"

The desk manager makes a pained smile, "Yes, sir."

"And while you're up there, we have noise complaints for room 813; can you stop by, tell them to knock it off?"

"Yes sir."

The manager almost walks away before he stops. "Oh, and, the McConnors party are wrapping up in Conference B, can you help Sharice put away the chairs?"

Tahir speaks like nails are being driven under his fingernails, "Uh—Yes-Yes, sir."

The clip-on cow chuckles, for my sake. "But, uh, worry about all this stuff when the line dies down, checking in customers comes first, of course, *hahaha.*"

Clip-on cow smiles at me like we are dear friends before he disappears.

Tahir, blinks hard. It is clear this job has shrunk his soul to the size of a mere pebble. He's been stunned. His diseased eyes stare vacantly at a computer screen.

"*Shedevry Kino,*" I say a fourth time, prodding him back into operation.

He gets me a key and tells me I'm on the top floor in room *904.*

"Our complimentary breakfast is served from six AM to—"

I walk away before he can continue speaking.

—

I find my room is of poor design. Everything is colored like champagne. A crooked picture hangs behind my bed of blonde children sprinting from a lighthouse.

I lay down my bag and stare at my reflection in a bubble television facing the bed.

I can hear New York out my windows. Six million screaming devils and their yellow taxi horns. I turn on the TV and turn the channel over to an infomercial for 1-800 number psychics who will help you win the lottery, and find missing loved ones.

Americans will believe anything.

—

I smoke cigarettes and prepare a dinner of ukha. The TV masks the noise of the city while the boiling fish and cabbage mask the city's stink.

I boil my soup in cheap pans from the room's private kitchen. Ukha is no gourmet meal, but I am convinced that any locally prepared food would land me in hospital.

When my meal is prepared I pour it into a bowl; it is a brownish brine, flecked with green parsley and chunks of white potato and nuggets of cheap salmon from a tin. It stinks like home. I will eat this same meal six times until it is time to return to Russia.

I ash my cigarette and arm myself with a spoon, but before I can take a bite, there is a knock on my door.

I recognize my visitor through the peephole. It is the man named Tahir in red velvet and bowtie. He is sweating. I open my door; and he smiles at me, so wide it seems as though he may collapse into death from the exertion.

"Mister Kino," he grins, joyless.

Kino is not my name. It's the last half of my company name and simply the Russian word for 'cinema,' but I do not correct him.

"I'm so sorry to bother you," he rasps, "Is your room to your liking?"

"Yes. Everything is fine—You can go."

I begin to shut the door before he stops me.

"Oh, oh, I'm afraid I do have to ask you a—*yes*—*sorry*—*uh*—*yes*— There have been several complaints from the other guests on this floor. Apparently they aren't happy with the smell of fish coming from your room here, and I'm afraid it's disturbing their sleep. Could we ask that you open a window?"

"No."

"Management would appreciate it if you would open a window and if in the future you refrained from cooking fish—If you'd like I can give you a coupon for the in-house dining menu—"

I take a '*Do Not Disturb*' sign from the nearby shelf and flaunt it to the man. Then I hang it on my door and slam it shut.

—

I eat my dinner and watch another infomercial for a cheap plastic product that poorly dices onions with a button. It can also chop nuts. Why anyone would want to be this is a conundrum to me. What drives Americans to fill their lives with so much junk?

I make two phone calls.

I call a secretary for Starikova to let him know I have arrived safely and that I am on schedule. I then call the translator for the film exchange. She tells me what time I can expect her at my hotel.

There is nothing more to do but preserve my energy. I sleep to the sound of information commercials.

—

The next morning I shower and I do push-ups. I consider a walk; but I do not wish to be assaulted or mugged. In truth I do not wish to see this city at all. I have no interest in green Statue of Liberty or the big candy store malls or any of the museums bragging about America's rape of the world. Starikova was sure to tell me of the great pleasures to be had here. That New York is one big carnival. He raved of dishes of deep fried pork and cheeses. Beer in oversized novelty jugs. Clubs full of feel good drugs and easy women—but I've seen enough of this tomfoolery at his compound.

Instead, I stand on my balcony and I watch the gray snow. It is harder today. It speckles at my ninth floor window before it turns black in the streets.

I chain smoke cigarettes and watch the vermin squiggle below, in and out of taxis and holes into the underground. It reminds me of watching an ant pile. I remember visiting the woods as a child and pissing on ant hills. I enjoyed watching all the ants panic. I wish I could take a piss now and drown the streets of Manhattan. Send all these devils running from their buildings.

I laugh. I blow smoke.

—

This hotel room is a prison, but I will be free soon.

For twelve grueling hours I sit at the end of my bed and watch TV. I listen to my electric jazz tapes. I do push-ups. When there is nothing left to do I stand naked before the mirror. I stare into the eyeballs tattooed over my nipples and the church steeples framed between them. Arms of skulls and knives and spiders. A cackling demon at the neckline.

My biography in black ink. The branding of my story. The road that took me from the streets to a room in a palace. To here in New York— and the tape that will fly home with me.

—

At long last, the sun sets. A gray cloud borrows its glow from the city and makes the sky look like one great television screen without a signal.

I receive a phone-call at nineteen-thirty hours. Right on schedule. The front desk tells me I have a guest and I tell them to send her up.

Moments later there is a knock at the door. I check myself one last time in the mirror. I make sure my shirt is well ironed. That no hairs are out of place in my shoulder-length slick-back. Finally, I put on bulky shield sunglasses.

When I open my door, my translator awaits me.

Vittoria wears a blouse and horse-riding trousers that are tight around her figure like an hourglass. The top is navy color blue with a pattern of white ponies. She wears Texas boots of cow leather. She is quite high fashion. She is like a girl from a magazine with her seventy-five dollar haircut and a face of symmetrical features.

"*Привет*," she says with a proud smile.

I say the same thing back to her.

She speaks to me in English, her accent is pitiful. "Good fortune— to find you here in—bigcity New York."

I don't care to sit around and play English lesson.

I speak to her in Russian, *"We have time to wait; the restaurant is not so far away—"* I point at a chair beside the bed. *"**Садитесь**."*

Vittoria is of interesting character; she speaks five languages and trades international art for her primary income, among other, less reputable, vocations. She is wealthy. She is young. She is what they call a globetrotter and what they call self-made. Many men pine for her, but not myself; I find her greatly ignorant. A girl who runs with wolves thinking them shepherd dogs.

Though I invited her to sit on a chair, she takes to laying on her stomach on my bed, legs kicking, shoulders arched like a cat begging for affection. I adjust my sunglasses and sit near her, stone faced. I do not give her the attention she so craves.

She is dark skinned and quite well fed and not so delicate for a woman. Her hair is chocolate gold and it is curly. Perhaps it is her eyes that are most interesting. They are the color of olives and honey. At times they make her seem like a witch of a storybook.

She again tries for English, bouncing her words as if to sing, *"He wears his sunglasses at night."*

She chuckles, I say nothing.

"It is a song," she explains, smacking my shoulder; suddenly she transitions to Russian, she is surprisingly adept at the language for a foreigner, *"How long have you been in America?"*

I tell her twenty-two hours.

"I landed an hour ago," she says. *"Plane travel has left me restless — do you have alcohol?"*

"Starikova has forbidden us from drinking any alcohol before this deal. He wants our senses keen."

Vittoria rolls her eyes like a spoiled teenager. "Starikova—" she changes to English, "Control Freak—" back to Russian. *"How is he? Every month now he is sending me a gift of some kind. Nesting Dolls. And clocks. And silk kerchiefs. It's all so sweet."*

"Pakhan Starikova is the devil," I tell her. *"He lives only for the suffering of others."*

Vittoria holds her nose up. *"This is just how he presents himself to his business associates. Beneath his exterior, he is a man of vision and passion. He is a revolutionary. The Russians are a repressed people; he understands the animal trapped inside the man; a beast of violence and lust and desire. He yearns to free the animal; to tell its story."*

"Animals have no stories to tell."

Starikova has long been enamored with Vittoria, just as she is with him. He speaks of her often and tells me of the wicked things he'd like to do to her. At times she is an object of his obsession and he will become quite enraged when she does not return his phone calls.

"Сигарета," Vittoria commands of me, snapping her fingers.

I hand off a cigarette and light it for her at her lips.

She rolls it around her fingers; I don't think she actually wants to smoke, she just wants something to play with. Ash rains onto my linen sheets as she hardly ever takes a genuine drag.

"Tell me about it," she inspects her unsmoked cigarette.

"Tell you about what?"

"The deal for which I am to serve translator—no one would discuss it on the phone—it is all so…" She pauses and then switches to English, "Cloak and dagger."

I watch the TV. Car chase in southern American woods.

She continues to press me, *"All I know is Big Boss Starikova is renting a new movie from the Zalatoris? Tonight we are to visit the world's most expensive—eh—*Blockbuster Video? *So, what is this movie he wants to see so bad?"*

I say nothing.

"Must be some special movie to fly the both of us to New York city."

I say nothing, still.

And she pesters me, *"You're awful quiet. Nervous? Tell me, is it a horror movie Starkova is buying? Are you a—eh— scaredy cat?"*

"Tonight's meeting is for the purchase and transfer of a snuff film," I tell her. "**Черная видеокассета.**"

"I had assumed this—D'uh," she rolls her eyes.

Of all the things I have done for Pakhan Starikova, none are as vile as those actions I have commit to obtain him his *black tapes*.

Starikova is an avid collector of snuff films. They are his most prized possessions. He keeps them in a safe with his paper cash holdings. These are tapes of accidents. War training films. Videos of performance stunts gone wrong. Even films seized by police of pervert serial killers. Mere ownership of these films is an offense worthy of imprisonment in Russia, but this has never slowed him down.

He watches his black tapes in private, for inspiration and pleasure alike. Sometimes, if he's had enough to drink, Starikova will put on these horrid films to shock his house guests at dinner parties. Vittoria was in attendance for one such incident. She was translating a dinner with the Zalatoris' at Starikova's palace compound when he abruptly put a black tape on; horrible movie of Russian teenager being tied to a tree by a gang of men. While the other Italians vomited or ran from the room, Vittoria watched quietly with a finger tapping upon her chin. She watched all nineteen minutes— of innocent child being played with like a toy and ultimately disposed of with fire. When it ended, she told Starikova the piece was **Насильственное искусство**; *brutal art*. She even dared to call it brave.

"*What is this one about?*" she asks me.

"*Starikova tells me it's the worst one money can buy.*"

Her eyes twinkle, a sadistic excitement, "*Yes—and?*"

"*I have already told you all the information I am privy to.*"

"*But surely you know something of its contents? A clue? Is it a movie star death tape? A celebrity autopsy? Is it the video from the man with the horses? The one he has sought so long?*"

I say nothing.

"*You must know something,*" she pleads, she says my name with hand on the crook of my elbow. "*Where's the video from? What happens in it? How did the Zalatoris' get their hands on it?*"

"*You should not show excitement for such dreadful materials; they are cigarettes for the soul. They will turn your heart black.*"

"*I beg you; tell me something—*"

I weigh the silence. I gaze at the carpet at the end of my boots; filthy. The color of stray dogs.

"*I can tell you this: Pakhan Starikova has sought this video for some time; a black tape of profound filth. It is said the content is so shocking, that when one views it, their hair will turn white before the film's end— this is all I know. I can say no more.*"

"**Захватывающий!**" she says, she references the VHS player sitting atop the bed. "*Perhaps we will have to have a—er—*sneak peek—*before you take it back to Russia.*"

"*I do not watch such films,*" I tell her. "*Not if it is by choice.*"

She makes an '*aw*' noise, the sound a person might make to reference a puppy or kitten, then asks me if I'm **Мальчик** as she laughs loudly and shakes my shoulder.

—

I fuck Vittoria if only because it kills twenty minutes. Neither of us undress, nor do we kiss. I simply lower her trousers and take her standing, leaning over the bed. It is simple and quick and dispassionate, but somehow it seems necessary. Some natural consequence of her private company.

When it is over, Vittoria and I smoke cigarettes. We watch information commercials; one is for a cockroach trap. It is a platform of sugar and glue with a plastic cover over it. They call it a *roach motel*. A cartoon roach crawls in and the next shot reveals him with X's over his eyes.

When it is twenty-three hundred hours, Vittoria and I leave the hotel. We walk gangland streets of chipped brick buildings and brown snow and honking yellow taxi cabs. There are many people out due to the Christmas time season—and because Vittoria is so beautiful and has large breasts, there are many men who stare at us. I feel like she is a target upon my back. It makes me feel as though I am walking through a jungle and all the hungry beasts are following us to pounce.

"A beautiful night!" Vittoria says to me, in English.

I have nothing to say.

A car slows down beside us and a man lobs himself out the passenger window. He shouts some obscenity, but it is said too quickly for me to understand it.

"Fucka—your mother!" Vittoria blasts back in return as they drive away.

She walks closer to me after this.

—

We travel fifteen blocks to the southside of Manhattan. We arrive at an upscale restaurant and butchery called Fortunado's. It is a fifty year old business in ownership of gangsters associated with the Zalatoris. We find it situated at the end of Little Italy with front windows boasting the severed heads of pigs and skinned rabbits.

Vittoria and I enter the establishment. Fortunado's is quite opulent. Over mirrored floors of chessboard pattern, Americans eat freshly slaughtered pork and house-made noodles. They swill large glasses of beer and grape wine. The young people somehow seem artificial, like wax statues; they are made of stage make-up and special undergarments that shape their bodies to seem more food-starved. The old people appear sick. They are bloated and red from their American dairy and lifetime of smoggy air.

A young girl awaits us at a wooden podium. She is small. She wears a black tie and a man's shirt.

"Hi, I'm so sorry, the kitchen has just closed. I'm afraid we're not seating new tables."

Vittoria snaps, she speaks like her words are meant for a slave, "We have private party with Palo."

"Oh! Of course, right this way!"

—

The hostess takes us past the dining area and its gameboard floors. We soon go through a bustling kitchen where brown men with hairy arms cook meat and wash dishes to the tune of rock and roll music. We are only here but a moment, soon we pass through a back door, and down a grim, stone staircase. This bottoms out at a frozen meat locker and basement butchery.

Like the subway exits, this is another hallway of white tiles and green light, only here, instead of movie posters, the walls are lined with headless and halved pigs on hooks in the mist of refrigeration vents.

The hostess guides us to a door at the meat locker's rear; but she takes us no further.

Vittoria makes no hesitation. She opens the door.

Here, beyond the butchery, is a small office. A hang-out spot for card games and contraband storage. The room is hardly more than a couch and a card table. It is lit by a lone light bulb that hangs from the ceiling over a ratty twine carpet. The walls are stacked with crates of newly imported VHS. Some of the Zalatori's micro-budget Gialo.

Two men await us.

"Vittoria!" Palo sings. "*Bella cara, Vittoria.*"

Palo Zalatori hops from his seat at the card table and embraces our translator, putting her breasts square against his gold cross necklace. They kiss each other's cheeks. He must say something charming in his half Spanish, half French, cow language. It makes her laugh so hard she has to clutch her chest.

Palo Zalatori is from Naples. He is excitable like a Chihuahua dog. He boasts long California surfer hair and wears a low cut suede shirt the color of cotton candy.

He is accompanied by a bald man in a black hat. This man does not stand up to greet us. He is large and has a face of flesh burns and scars. I assume him to be nothing but the muscle. Perhaps a body man himself. He eats a dinner of tomato sauce and gray veal.

Palo comes to me and butchers the Russian language while shaking his hands in the air, "Privyy-yet—e Correcto?—er—Doba—dobaryy Vetcha—vetcher."

He sings this gibberish with the excitement of a schoolboy. I say nothing. I sit down at the card table with folded hands. The Bald Man In The Black Hat acknowledges me with the tip of veal at the end of his fork. He then buries it in his teeth.

"Let's be—uh—getting straight down to'the businesses, huh?" Palo cheers in pitiful English.

He sits. Vittoria sits. Our chairs are cheap and squeak loudly.

Palo wastes no time romancing Vittoria; he hangs an arm around her neck and chews on her ear with small talk in impenetrable Italian. She giggles. *Fermata,* she tells him.

Eventually, I find Palo Zalatoi speaking directly at me.

Vittoria translates into Russian, *"Er—Palo asks if your hotel is to your liking?"*

"Tell him I do not wish to make small talk. I wish to begin our dealings."

The Zalatori family are clowns. They made their money in the sixties moving heroin from Middle East to the New York ports, but somewhere along the way became a bogus film studio not unlike Shedevry Kino. We would not do business with them if Starikova was not so fond of their dirty movies. The Zalatori Production Company produces garbage horror movies on shoestring budgets, films about forest beasts and cannibals and motorcycle terror gangs. Since 1978 Palo Zalatori's father has produced nearly thirty-two films. Spaghetti sauce movies whose production launder very real blood money.

Palo suddenly turns serious, he snaps his fingers twice. On cue, The Bald Man in The Black Hat sets down his fork. He reaches into his breast pocket and out it comes—the VHS film.

The very black tape I have been sent here to retrieve. He sets it gently at the table's center before returning to his dish to loudly slurp noodles.

It's an ordinary brick of black plastic. It has viewing windows to white spools of reflective metal tape. On the back are two plastic gears; they stare upon me, like eyes. A label is on the front, in pen it reads squiggly gibberish I have no hope to understand.

"E ora il dolce!" Palo is ever so flamboyant; "Film-a pazzesco! Film-a selvaggio! L'capo Starikova lo adorerà!"

Vittoria gets to translating to Russian, "*The movie is— it will be the pride of Boss Starikova's collection.*"

I nod. Slowly. Palo has a reputation for overselling his work.

Palo babbles on; he must rapid-fire twenty words a second. Vittoria struggles to keep up with him.

"*He says the tape is—er—it does not translate—film di donna sulla sedia—a 'woman in chair film.' He says the woman is quite striking in her beauty. She is tied down. There are—many men—and they, er, violate the woman for about an hour with her, a variety of tools as she—gives much blood.*"

Palo keeps talking and Vittoria narrates over him, struggling at times to keep up.

"*There is uh, play with the butt, er—he says there's scenes—of strangulation—of—horror—but, truly it is the woman's beauty and her desire to live that make it such the quality picture that it is. To witness such suffering, in such detail, it is a treat Boss Starikova will remember for all his years.*"

Palo says his last piece. He makes pizza-pasta gibberish then grins wide and explodes his hands outwards.

"*She is so full of life,*" Vittoria translates. "*Her slow death is an explosion of misery.*"

I tell her to tell them that I agree.

"*That doesn't make sense,*" she tells me. "*You can't just tell them you agree. You haven't seen his movie. Did you misunderstand me? Did I mistranslate something?*"

"*Tell them: 'I agree,' Vittoria.*"

She does. Palo then mutters to the man with the burned face. He shrugs and eats a noodle.

I feel weak having all of my words go through a translator, so, I speak to these clowns in English, the only language we all halfway speak. "It. Has. To Be. The Best. Movie. Ever made—Or—Starikova—makes no more—deals—ever again."

Palo raises his hands, he says something to Vittoria.

She translates, "*He assures you, it is.*"

"*Tell them I did not fly 2000 miles to hear empty promises.*"

She does. They telephone back more rubbish about how great their '*Woman in Chair*' film is.

"*Ask them about the specifications.*"

She telephones, then telephones back, "*He, er, wants to know what do you mean 'specifications'?*"

I clarify, "*The camera and sound equipment. The lighting quality. Pakhan Starikova wants high-definition. High fidelity or there is no purchase.*"

The prompt is filtered through Vittoria; Palo speaks all about the lights and the brand of microphone. As last details, Vittoria informs me that Palo operates the camera himself and he has a long resume as a cinematographer.

I nod once more. My shield sunglasses fall down the bridge of my nose so I pull them back up. The three Italians look to me, inspecting their own warped reflections in my lenses.

I lean in and ask Vittoria's left ear, "*Ask them their price.*"

She poses the question to Palo. Palo puts words into her right ear and gives them back to me.

"*To obtain a special item—like this—he is requesting—a high price. He asks that you consider his personal risk taken to obtain the film and the great lengths the Zalatori's have gone to please Boss Starikova in the past—*"

I interrupt; "*—Enough. Tell him to give me a price.*"

She says this to Palo and she returns a moment later to repeat his words, "*Three Hundred Thousand American dollars—Hold on.*"

Vittoria and Palo argue, as they do, their hands pinch at the air. I find myself bored. I regard The Bald Man In The Black Hat. He eats the last of his veal puck as he maintains an eager focus to Vittoria's chest.

"*Sorry—*" Vittoria apologizes to me. "*—I thought he misspoke—the price is three hundred thousand American dollars.*"

"*Tell him that's agreeable.*"

Her honey olive eyes pop. She doesn't translate, instead she asks me, "*Are you sure? That is a high price for a single movie—it is just a tape.*"

"*It is a black tape. The best ever made. There is no price too high for Starikova. Say this to Palo. Every word.*"

I nod to Palo, a soft drop of the nose. She translates Starikova's sentiments and Palo grins. Then, the Italian reaches out to shake my hand.

We shake and The Bald Man In The Black Hat drops his fork.

—

There is a small window beyond the card table, it is where the wall meets the ceiling. It looks out at the street level. I watch the high heels and penny loafers of rich, drunk Americans as they scramble for yellow color taxi cabs in the steadily rising snow. Above us, where there was once the sound of rock music and chefs, there is now a heavy silence. The place has emptied out after closing time and the air has filled with the sound of hissing refrigerator pumps from the nearby meat-locker. This and the noise of faraway traffic on Broadway.

The Bald Man In The Black Hat leaves us. There is only myself, Palo and Vittoria. We discuss the trivial details of how we will arrange for the exchange of the cash. But once these details are finalized, we shake hands once more.

Palo beams, "Ora che abbiamo finito, possiamo festeggiare!"

"*What did he say?*" I ask.

Vittoria switches to her pitiful English. "Now, the deal is done, we have a party!"

The Bald Man In The Black Hat returns to the room, careful to only poke his head in.

Palo asks him, "Il ristorante è vuoto?"

"All empty," The Bald Man In The Black Hat confirms.

Palo smiles at Vittoria, but gives his command to his servant, "Prendi lo champagne, vero?"

"Al momento. Al Momento."

The Bald Man in The Black takes the cue. He disappears once more.

"Un momento!" Palo grins at us as he stands up, he wags a finger. "Un momento! Attendere qui!"

Soon he disappears too, pinching the skin of my neck three times on his way out the door.

Vittoria and I are alone again; a three hundred thousand dollar VHS tape sits on its backside before us. I take it up, into my hands. It's so light. It's so—*empty.* Black plastic and magnets. Components of gears and plastic switches. A cursive title on the front, *Donna Sulla Sedia.* Just thinking of its contents make me wish to weep—but Pakhan Starikova will be pleased and I will make a handsome sum from this deal.

Vittoria snaps her fingers at me, "***Сигарета.***"

I take out my cigarette pack. She kisses a fresh stick and I light it for her.

I remark, "**каждую затяжку тяни, как последнюю. Это может быть твоя последняя сигарета в жизни.**"

"*A funny thing to say.*"

"*Something they used to say when we were kids in the warehouse.*"

After her first drag she stares at the tape with a bored expression.

Smoke exits her nostrils, "*So, the world's greatest snuff film, it's all yours now.*"

"*It is Pakhan Starikova's—*"

She touches my shoulder. *"Three hundred thousand! Must be some gorgeous woman in that chair."*

I have no response to this. I stare at the tape. I think of Hell.

"Let us see about that champagne," I say.

Vittoria and I stand from the card table.

I walk behind her as we exit the backroom and return to the basement butchery.

As we enter the tile floor butchery, Vittoria is surprised to discover that the room has been rearranged. The split-belly pigs have been gathered off to one side. Where there was once a walkway there is now an empty dentist's chair sat in the center of the room. A table nearby is situated with duct tape, and hand-cuffs—a drill—a hammer. Lastly, a high end VHS camera is situated on a tripod, affixed with a flashlight and directional microphone. It faces the chair. Its motor softly hums. A red light blinks a dozen times a second.

Vittoria stammers. Her cigarette falls out of her mouth and goes bouncing at her heels. She examines each of us, one at a time, but our faces offer no explanation. No comfort. No answers.

The Bald Man In The Black Hat locks the door to the upstairs.

Palo locks the door to the meeting room.

I load the blank VHS into the open, awaiting, slot of the camera.

HORRORMAXX: VOL. 1

By. H.T. Boyd

Cover Illustration cat by @lupsdesign, logo and layout by H.T.B.

At no point in the creation of this book was Artificial Intelligence used to generate written content including dialogue, plots, or word styling.

In the instance of this particular work, Artificial Intelligence *was* used for translation purposes in the story '*Woman in Chair Film*'.

Novels by H.T. Boyd:

Leutogi: A Horror Story

Palo Duro: A Sci-Fi Story

Go You And Touch That Beautiful Black: A Detective Story

HORRORMAXX Vol. 1

HORRORMAXX Vol. 2

Version 1.24

Copyright © 2024 H.T. BOYD

All Rights Reserved

ISBN: 979-8-9911058-0-4